NEVER SURRENDER

Foreword

NEVER SURRENDER was first published by the U.K. publisher Hodder and Stoughton as A PIECE OF RESISTANCE in 1970. I had originally called it THE HUNDRED YEARS WAR because when asked how long the Resistance was prepared to go on fighting, Garnett, the hero, replies 'Five, ten, twenty, fifty or even a hundred years.' This title was quickly dropped when Robin Denniston, the then editorial director of Hodders, told me they were publishing a book on the Salvation Army with the same title.

A PIECE OF RESISTANCE was written in my spare time when I was an Instructor at the School of Infantry. While it was intended to be merely an entertainment, the book does contain a number of observations, particularly as regards the semi hostile attitude of the population at large towards the Resistance after four years of Soviet occupation.

The book saw the light of day thanks to my agent, the late George Greenfield, who nursed me through six other unpublishable novels. By the time I delivered the seventh he must have felt he was nursing a turkey. However, George subsequently told me that he became so engrossed in the story that he hadn't realised his pipe was still alight when he tucked it away in his jacket pocket and eventually set himself on fire.

Clive Egleton © 2004

NEVER SURRENDER

Clive Egleton

This title first published in Great Britain 2004 by
SEVERN HOUSE PUBLISHERS LTD of
9–15 High Street, Sutton, Surrey SM1 1DF.
First published in 1970 in Great Britain by Hodder and Stoughton
under the title *A Piece of Resistance.*
This title first published in the USA 2004 by
SEVERN HOUSE PUBLISHERS INC of
595 Madison Avenue, New York, N.Y. 10022.

British Library Cataloguing in Publication Data

Egleton, Clive, 1927-
    Never surrender
    1.   Insurgency - Great Britain - Fiction
    2.   Military occupation - Great Britain - Fiction
    3.   Alternative histories
    4.   Suspense fiction
    I.   Title
    823.9'14 [F]

    ISBN 0-7278-6059-3

Printed and bound in Great Britain by
MPG Books Ltd., Bodmin, Cornwall.

1

It was one of those cold, grey days in mid-March when the chill in the air cuts right through to the bone and dispels any notion that spring is only just around the corner.

As he left the shelter of the tube station, Pollard turned up the collar of his overcoat, and stepped out briskly along the high street. It was comparatively empty considering the time of day, and this was a blessing so far as he was concerned, because it made it that much more difficult for anyone to follow him.

After covering thirty metres, he suddenly turned on his heel and retraced his steps as far as the tobacconist's in the station arcade where he bought a packet of cigarettes from a vending machine, and, satisfied that he was not being followed, he then crossed the road and made his way back along the high street.

The garage looked as if the owner was on the verge of bankruptcy. Only one car was on display in the showroom, and if there was a salesman on the staff he wasn't evident. Of six petrol pumps in the forecourt, five were labelled out of order. Pollard crossed the forecourt, walked round to the back of the garage and entered the workshops.

The smart, blue, Austin 1800 in the out inspection bay met with his approval. It was the sort of car he favoured, because it was discreet enough not to attract attention and yet powerful enough for his needs. Raising the bonnet, he laid a hand on the radiator cap.

A voice behind him said, "It isn't hot."

Turning quickly, Pollard saw a small man in a crumpled blue serge suit loitering outside the door of the works office. He slammed the bonnet down and said, "How did you come by it?"

"Insurance company wrote it off after an accident, we rebuilt it."

5

"Any snags?" said Pollard following the man into his office.

"Chassis's out of line; a new set of tyres wouldn't last you more than six thousand."

"How about cornering?"

"No problem apart from it being heavy on the tyres."

Pollard closed the office door behind him. "I don't like the bit about the chassis," he said.

The man shrugged his shoulders. "These days we don't have much choice." He opened a drawer and brought out a poster which he pushed across the desk at Pollard. "This might interest you," he said.

The photograph was out of focus but even so it was apparent that it bore no resemblance to Pollard. The man was holding a set of numbers across his chest and looked suitably grave. Thinning fair hair, parted on the left, emphasised a bulging forehead. The caption underneath the photograph read, £100,000 Reward, Wanted for Murder, John Richard Seymour, alias John Evans, alias Richard Pollard.

Pollard put the poster to one side. "Do you find the offer tempting, Charlie?" he said quietly.

"You know it isn't. I'm worried because you're getting too hot for comfort."

"Who's going to recognise me from that photograph?"

"Nobody."

"Well there you are then."

"They have your name right, and somehow they connect you with the army. They just have a photograph of the wrong man, that's all."

Pollard leaned over the desk. "Charlie," he said softly, "we see this one job through together, and then we forget we ever met. Right?"

"If you say so."

"I say so. Now fill me in on the details."

"You've seen the car already, and like I said, it isn't hot. The kit you wanted is in a green holdall in the boot." Charlie swung round in the swivel chair and opened the cupboard behind him. Revolving to face Pollard once again, he placed a Gladstone bag on the desk.

6

"This is your trade mark, so to speak. Go ahead, take a look inside, any doctor would be proud to have one like it these days."

Pollard said, "I'll take your word for it. What about a sticker for the rear window?"

"There's one on it already."

Pollard smiled thinly. "And now all I want is a gun," he said.

Charlie got up out of his chair and went into the lavatory, leaving the door ajar. Pollard saw him stand on the seat, raise the lid of the cistern and fish around inside it until he found the oilskin packet.

"I'm disappointed in you, Charlie," he said sadly, "that's the first place the bogies would think of looking."

Charlie dropped the cistern lid back in place and came back into the office leaving a trail of water behind him. "I'll be glad to get rid of this," he said, dropping the wet bundle on to the desk.

Pollard unwrapped the oilskin and checked the Luger Automatic. The weapon had been well cared for and a light film of oil covered the working parts, which moved back smoothly as he snapped a round up into the breech. He unbuttoned his overcoat and jacket and slipped the gun into a hip holster. He adjusted his clothing, lit a cigarette and leaned back against the wall. The Cuban tobacco tasted and smelt foul.

The telephone jangled twice, stopped for a few seconds and then pealed once more. Charlie looked up from the now silent instrument, "That's it," he said, "they've gone into the bank."

Pollard glanced at his wristwatch. "Right on time too," he said. He opened the door, picked up the Gladstone bag and walked out of the office without another word.

He threw the bag on to the back seat, got into the Austin 1800 and started the engine, and ran it until he had warmed it up to the correct temperature. Pollard knew to the precise second how long it would take him to reach the Co-operative Bank in the Harrow Road, for he had planned this job with meticulous care.

As he drove along the high street, he went over the details in his mind searching for any tiny point which he might have overlooked. The Stantons were the only weak link in the plan, and there was nothing he could do about them. They were the only people available with anything like the right qualifications. Everything would be all right if they didn't fail him.

Jean Stanton unbuttoned her coat and leaned back in the chair. It was uncomfortably hot in Swainson's office with the central heating on full blast and the windows closed. She could feel the sweat trickling down between her breasts and she found it hard to breathe. Out of the corner of her eye, she could see that her husband was pale and tense.

She glanced at the clock on the wall above Swainson's head and saw that time was running out for them. Mentally she cursed Swainson for being such a cautious old maid that he felt it necessary to have Marshall, the assistant manager, holding his hand while he examined their request for a loan.

Pollard had assured her that the papers were in order and there would be no problem. Now, judging by the way Swainson was scrutinising their balance sheet, it was beginning to look as if there was a flaw in their cover story. Heart beating wildly and feeling sick, she leaned back in her chair and closed her eyes.

"Are you all right, Mrs Stanton?" Swainson asked anxiously.

Jean passed a hand across her forehead. "I feel a little sick," she said faintly.

"Perhaps a glass of water, Mr Marshall?" Swainson suggested.

Now, she thought, now while Marshall is out of the room, for Christ's sake do it now. She was aware that Swainson was half way out of his chair and leaning forward over the desk, his eyes fixed on her.

Stanton reached down into his open briefcase which lay by the side of his chair and whipped out a gas pistol. He pointed it straight into Swainson's face, as Pollard had instructed, and pulled the trigger.

The effect was immediate. Swainson opened his mouth to cry out but no sound came from his lips. Instinctively he clawed at his collar, and then, like a puppet, he reared back before slumping forward on to the desk. One arm jerked out and sent a glass ashtray crashing on to the floor.

Jean leapt to her feet, ran to the door and opened it. Her eyes

8

swept over the crowd of customers in the bank, and, locating Pollard amongst them, her confidence returned.

"Mr Marshall," she shouted, in a cracked voice, "please come quickly, something dreadful has happened to Mr Swainson."

A crowd of sheep-like faces gazed at her open mouthed and looked as though they were about to bleat in unison.

Pollard shouldered his way through. "I'm a doctor," he said loudly, "what seems to be the trouble?"

"In the office, it's Mr Swainson, he seems to have had some kind of a fit."

Pollard stopped in the door, and, facing about, spoke to the crowd. "It's all right," he said reassuringly, "there's nothing to be alarmed about."

He walked into the office and closed the door behind him. Pushing Marshall to one side, he bent over Swainson and checked his pulse. "I need my bag," he said crisply, looking up at Stanton. He tossed him a set of keys and said, "My car's outside, a blue Austin 1800. You'll also find a green holdall in the boot. I'd be grateful if you'd fetch both bags for me."

Marshall licked his lips nervously. "How is Mr Swainson?" he whispered.

"He's had a heart attack."

"Should I call an ambulance?"

"If you would," said Pollard, "the number of the nearest emergency station is 619547."

It seemed to Jean Stanton that by the way he so effortlessly lifted Swainson out of the chair and laid him full length on the floor, Pollard might well have been dealing with a child. From his manner, and the way he massaged Swainson's heart, she could almost believe he was medically qualified.

Marshall put the phone down. "The ambulance is on its way," he said hoarsely.

Pollard nodded his head and went on massaging Swainson's heart. The veins stood out on his forehead and the sweat poured down his face. He looked up and said, "For God's sake, someone open a window, it's stifling in here."

9

Marshall scuttled across the office and fiddled with the latch on the window. He succeeded in opening it as Stanton returned carrying the holdall and the Gladstone bag.

Without a word, Pollard stood up, took the Gladstone out of Stanton's hand and laid it on the desk. He opened the bag and took out a syringe and a bottle of colourless fluid. As he filled the hypodermic from the bottle, Pollard said, "I'll have to stimulate the heart."

He knelt down again and swabbed Swainson's chest and then gave him the injection. Laying the syringe to one side, he started to massage the heart again. In the silence of the office, they heard a siren wail in the distance.

Marshall licked his lips again. "I think that must be the ambulance," he said nervously, and then inconsequentially, he added, "I can't think how it could have happened; I'd only just left the office to fetch Mrs Stanton a glass of water and Mr Swainson looked so fit and well."

Pollard ignored him. He stopped massaging, and, putting his ear close to Swainson's chest, listened for a heart beat. Jean noticed that he looked concerned and the thought flashed through her mind that something had gone wrong.

The door opened and a voice said; "Shall I bring the stretcher in here, Doctor?"

Pollard looked up and nodded. He got to his feet slowly and in a grave voice said, "I'm afraid this man is dead."

The words hung like a thunderclap in the still air. Marshall's mouth fell open like a stranded fish. Stanton's face was the colour of putty.

"Had Mr Swainson a wife?" Pollard asked gently.

The Adam's apple bobbed up and down in Marshall's throat as he struggled to get the words out. "She lives in the flat above," he said eventually.

Pollard closed the bag and picked it up. "I think we had better break the news to her," he said. He turned to Jean, "Perhaps you would come with us, Mrs Stanton. I think she will need a woman's sympathy at a time like this. If you would lead the way, Mr

10

Marshall?" Glancing back at Stanton, he said, "Would you mind bringing the holdall with you."

A drama critic could not have faulted Pollard. He was quietly authoritative and had exactly the right blend of compassion but firm persuasion. With the minimum of fuss, he cleared a way through the crowd for the ambulance men and prodded Marshall into leading them round to the Swainson's flat.

Mrs Swainson was in her early forties, a small pleasant looking woman with a round plumpish face. The smile on her face froze when she saw the four of them on her doorstep and heard the ambulance moving off in the background. Her hand flew to her mouth, "It's James, isn't it?" she whispered.

Marshall said miserably, "This gentleman is a doctor, Mrs Swainson. He did all he could."

Pollard pushed his way past Marshall and took hold of her arm. "He wasn't in any pain," he said in a soothing voice.

Her face crumpled and broke and the tears streamed down her cheeks as Pollard led her up the staircase. "It's all right, Mr Marshall," he called back, "this lady and gentleman will help me to look after her."

"Oh God," she moaned, "Oh God, how could you? Oh James. Oh God, Oh my God."

Pollard led her into a bedroom and gently forced her down into an easy chair. He opened the bag, took out another syringe, and then pushed up the sleeve of her woollen dress. "It's going to be all right," he said kindly, "just something to make you sleep." He jabbed the needle into a vein.

"No," she said wildly, "you mustn't, who's going to meet Andy from school?" Her eyes clouded over, and her tongue lolled out of her mouth.

"What have you done to her?" Jean shouted.

Pollard whipped round and clapped a hand over her mouth. "It's just a shot of Pentathol to keep her quiet," he said, "now for God's sake get a hold on yourself. You'll have the bogies kicking the door in before we know where we are."

He waited until he was sure that she had calmed down before he

11

removed his hand.

Stanton said, and there was a note of hysteria in his voice, "You swore to me that no harm would come to him."

"What makes you think anything has happened to him?"

"He'd stopped breathing, hadn't he?"

"So what if he had? The boys in the ambulance will try to resuscitate him. He has better than a fifty fifty chance." -

"You mean there's a chance he really might die?" Jean said quickly.

"There is that chance," Pollard admitted.

"You're mad," Stanton said hoarsely.

"I had no choice. I had to be sure of getting into this flat and staying here."

"You're not after the bank, are you, Pollard?"

"You're so right. In less than ten minutes from now, Edwin Blythe, our Home Secretary and Minister for Internal Security is going to come riding down the High Street right past this flat in his armour plated Rolls Royce, and I am going to kill him."

"And for that, I may have killed an innocent man."

"In a war," Pollard said coldly, "innocent people are killed every day, and make no mistake we are fighting a war."

"I'm not having any part in this assassination."

"I'm not asking you to. You take your wife and get out of here. Nobody will see you if you leave by the kitchen door. There is a gate at the bottom of the garden which leads into the alleyway behind the station. Go through the station to the car park where you'll find a blue Cortina, licence number HKA 592B. There's five hundred pounds in the glove compartment. Take the car and drive out to the Load of Hay on the Guildford By-pass. Tell the landlord you've been recommended by Cromwell."

"Just what are you trying to pull?" Stanton said fiercely.

"A safe route out of the country for the pair of you with ten thousand dollars standing to your credit in the Chase National Bank, New York." Pollard took a key out of his pocket and tossed it to Stanton. "You'll need this," he said, "it's the key to the Cortina. Now get the hell out of here."

12

For a moment Stanton hesitated, and then he grabbed Jean by the arm and dragged her out of the room.

Pollard said, "Don't make any phone calls, you're being watched."

"What the hell makes you think I'll waste time on a phone call?" Stanton shouted from the kitchen.

The back door slammed behind them and suddenly the flat was quiet. Pollard glanced at the unconscious woman in the chair and then picked up the green holdall. He went through into the lounge and opened the side window carefully.

From his vantage point, Pollard could see the railway bridge one hundred and fifty metres away. Turning away from the window he peeled off his overcoat and laid it on the back of a convenient chair. He undid the holdall and removed an RPG 7, a free flight missile which was capable of stopping a medium tank. He drew up a chair and sat facing the window, nursing the RPG 7 on his lap while he waited for Blythe to appear in view.

He sat there at the window thinking about Blythe, a jumped up Third Secretary in the Beirut Embassy who had defected to Moscow in the early sixties, and who had returned to England with the Soviet Occupation Forces. As Minister for Internal Security, Blythe controlled the Special Branch and the National Police Force, and was considered to be the most forceful personality in the Cabinet. His death would shake the Puppet Government to the core.

Pollard was spared a long wait. The beat of the Norton exhausts alerted him a few seconds before he saw the car. There were seven motor cycle outriders preceding the Rolls-Royce in an inverted V formation, and he lined up the car in the optic sight as it came over the bridge and turned into the high street.

At one hundred metres he could pick out Blythe's features clearly; at seventy-five he could see the colour of the tie around his neck, at fifty metres he opened fire and the car disintegrated in a gout of flame. Two sack-like objects soared up into the air before falling back on to the road where they lay smouldering. In the confusion, an outrider mounted the pavement and crashed into the plate glass window of a furniture department.

13

Pollard dropped the launcher, grabbed his coat and ran out of the room into the kitchen. He tried to open the back door but it wouldn't budge, and it slowly dawned on him that Stanton must have locked it on the outside. In desperation he put his shoulder to the door but the lock held, and, reluctantly, he gave it up as a bad job and returned to the hall.

He dropped his coat on the floor, and picking up the phone from the hall table, dialled the number he wanted. Holding the instrument in one hand, he slipped the Luger out of the hip holster and stood watching the door.

He spoke calmly and deliberately into the mouthpiece, even as he heard the sound of jackboots on the staircase outside. He finished talking as the front door splintered under an axe.

2

In Garnett's opinion, Crescent House was a twelve storied monstrosity of concrete, steel and glass designed by a mentally retarded architect. The firm of Cobb, Coleman, and Varley occupied the fourth floor and his office was, relatively speaking, the size of a hen coop in a battery layer.

He stood by the window looking out towards the GPO Tower, and the Soviet flag which flew above it. The Russians didn't use the tower but their flag flew on the masthead simply because it was the biggest landmark in London, and it was therefore a forceful reminder to the population that they were living in an occupied city.

Garnett was not the most successful solicitor in the firm partly because he had entered the profession in his late thirties but largely because he wasn't really interested in it. Conveyancing bored him to tears but it was a way of earning a living.

He was thirty-six years old and his black hair was beginning to fleck with grey. Over six foot tall and weighing one hundred and seventy-five pounds, he looked anything but a solicitor. He had a strong, square-shaped face and cold blue-grey eyes which hinted at a streak of ruthlessness. As far as his secretary, Valerie Dane, was concerned he was an enigma.

Dane was blonde, twenty-six years old, five foot seven and single. At one time she had seriously considered taking up modelling as a career, but, in an era where beanpoles were popular, she had too much flesh on her for regular employment. She became a secretary because at least she could put a desk between herself and her employer whereas the majority of photographers she had worked with merely wanted to get her on the couch in double quick time.

Garnett puzzled her because, despite the fact she had been closely associated with him for nearly a year, she hardly knew a thing about him. So far as his private life was concerned, he was as communicative as a mute. She assumed he wasn't married because she had no evidence to suppose otherwise.

She didn't like to admit it but his indifference annoyed her. Dane resented being treated like a piece of office furniture and that was exactly the way he did treat her. One day, she promised herself, one day she was going to make him sit up and take notice, and when that happened, she was going to lead him a dog's life.

Garnett turned away from the window. "Where did we get to?" he asked.

Dane crossed a pair of shapely legs while she consulted her pad. Finding the place, she said; "We have of course consulted Messrs Cleve and Richards who are representing Mr Norton. In our opinion, it is extremely difficult to say, with any certainty, where the dry rot first occurred." She looked up and waited for Garnett to resume.

The office intercom bleeped and a voice said, "Mr Garnett, Mr Coleman would like to see you in his office immediately, please." The machine went dead before Garnett had a chance to reply. He smiled at Dane and said; "HMV. I doubt if there will be time to finish the rest of the letter today; we'll leave it over for the morning."

She got up and straightened her skirt in a way which he thought was intended to draw his attention to her legs, and it amused him to give the impression that he hadn't noticed. He skirted the desk, opened the door for her and then went into Coleman's office.

Coleman was sixty-three, overweight, and in poor physical shape. Dandruff lay on the lapels of his suit like a thin covering of snow. He was also a chronic asthmatic and the green-coloured inhaler which he kept handy on his desk was in constant use.

He waved Garnett to a chair.

"This," he said patting the tape recorder on his desk, "just arrived by special delivery."

He punched the playback button, the tape hissed silently, a telephone rang several times and then there was a distinct clunk as

16

the receiver was lifted. A harsh voice, speaking calmly in measured tones said; "This is Pollard. The job was a success but I think the Stantons have gone across. Get reception to take care of them. They know about Cromwell, so pass the word to our people down there. I don't think I will be calling you again."

The connection was broken and a woman said dispassionately, "Message timed at twelve thirty-three."

Coleman punched the stop button. "Well?" he wheezed.

Garnett said: "I wonder if Pollard has been killed."

"I find myself hoping that might be the case."

"Isn't that a pretty callous attitude to take?"

You have to be callous in this business. We could be in serious trouble if they have taken Pollard alive."

Coleman didn't elaborate but that was typical of him. He had the habit of stating a fact and then leaving you to draw your own conclusions. Sometimes his tone of voice would indicate the lines on which he was thinking, but in this instance it was no help at all.

Garnett said; "Pollard seems to be in some doubt about the Stantons. He is not definite, he says he thinks they have gone across. I wonder why he said that?"

"You may," Coleman said, between deep breaths, "know the answer to that question when you find them."

Garnett drummed his fingers on the arm of the chair. "You want me to take care of them?"

"Correct."

"What do we know about them?"

"Very little," said Coleman. "Pollard didn't believe in keeping records." He picked up the inhaler and squirted it in his mouth. "They ran a bookshop, 24 The Arcade, South Ruislip; it's near the tube station."

"What else?"

"Nothing."

"Nothing?" Garnett echoed. "These people have over four hours' start on us, and you expect me to find them on that kind of information?" He pulled at the lobe of his left ear. "Have our people in Guildford been warned?"

17

"So I'm led to believe."

"Forget the Stantons then, sit tight and trust to luck."

"I'm afraid that won't do, we can't afford to close the Guildford route. We also have to salvage what we can from the mess. There is a possibility that the Stantons may have been in contact with other cells. If that is so, they could do us a great deal of harm if they talked to the wrong people."

Garnett rubbed his chin. "I'm going to need some help. I want a watch kept on the Guildford rendezvous in case Stanton does follow his instructions, and I'll have to get in touch with Endicott."

Coleman said; "I think we ought to leave Endicott well alone."

"I have to know what the police are doing, and only Endicott can tell me that. I know he is no longer on speaking terms with us, but he'll have to put up with us just this one more time. I shall have to get inside that bookshop too," Garnett scowled, "I don't like it, it could be dangerous."

Coleman unwrapped a cigar and trimmed it carefully with a silver penknife. "I don't want any attention drawn to this place," he said as he struck a match. He puffed on the cigar and watched the smoke drift towards the ceiling. "Do I make myself clear?"

"Absolutely."

"Good. Keep in touch, won't you?"

"Of course." Garnett stood up and walked to the door. Over his shoulder he said, "I may need petrol coupons, travel permits, cash, that sort of thing."

"You know where to get them," Coleman said dismissing him.

It was getting dark when Garnett drew into the lay-by facing the arcade. There was a delivery van parked outside the butcher's shop on the opposite side of the street, where it had been presumably left for the night, but otherwise there was nothing to arouse his suspicion. This absence of activity, plus the fact that there had been no significant traffic on the police band, which he had monitored on the car radio for the past hour, made him feel a little easier.

Garnett left the Hillman and went into a newsagent where he bought an evening paper. The coverage of the assassination was on the sparse side, possibly because the authorities wanted to keep the

18

Resistance in the dark about the line they were taking.

He tucked the newspaper under his arm and walked briskly to the call box on the corner. Slipping inside the booth, he turned up the telephone directory and checked to see if Stanton was listed. He glanced across the street at the bookshop and saw a light come on in the flat above and a woman appeared briefly in the window to draw the curtains. Garnett lifted the receiver and dialled Stanton's number. He waited until the phone had rung half a dozen times, broke the connection and then rang again. There was no answer.

Garnett hung up for the second time, left the call box and went back to the car. He started up and drove out on to the main road and then turned right into a side street beyond the arcade, where he parked the car again and got out.

The street lights came on but it was fairly dark in the alley behind the arcade. He tried the latch on the back gate, and, finding that it opened easily, he slipped inside the yard and stood in the shadows.

A flight of concrete steps led to the flat above, and there was a light burning in the kitchen upstairs. The door opened, a woman stood framed in the entrance and the faint sound of a radio, playing in the background, reached his ears. It seemed to him that she was staring into the patch of darkness where he was standing.

"Tibby, come on Tibby, come to mummy," she cooed, "you's a nice pussy." There was a short pause and then she said; "All right, stay outside and see if I care."

The sudden clatter of the dustbin lid made him jump. The woman replaced the lid and went back inside the kitchen, closing the door behind her. A train clattered noisily over the bridge, and a series of blue-white flashes lit the evening sky.

Something soft brushed against his legs, and Garnett looked down into a pair of yellow eyes. The cat rubbed itself against him and mewed loudly. He remained quite still, and, the cat losing interest in him, moved away and bounded up the flight of steps. It scratched impatiently at the back door and howled plaintively. The door opened a fraction and the cat slid inside with the assistance of a slippered foot which helped it on its way.

He waited for another five minutes to see if there would be any

19

further developments and then moved quickly across the yard and hid beneath the flight of steps. The door facing him presented no problem and he picked the lock easily. Stepping inside, he found himself in a small room, which, as his eyes accustomed to the dark, he saw was the kitchenette.

The premises contained a bedroom, a lounge—dining room and the shop. Working on the assumption that Stanton might have been operating a Dead Letter Box for Pollard, Garnett started with the shop.

It was not an easy task because he could not risk using his flash and the orange light given off from the street lamps was no help. The stock consisted of second hand hardbacks, paperbacks, and any number of pin up magazines. A random check disclosed that the second hand books had a musty smell about them and the magazines contained an unusually high proportion of vacuous women sporting over-developed busts whose normal attire, whether in an office, or washing up at the sink or flicking a duster about the house, appeared to be confined to panties, stockings, shoes and damn all else. Such business records that Garnett found were straightforward enough and a search of the floor and walls failed to reveal any secret hiding place.

Garnett gave up. He went into the lounge and drew the curtains. He took a pencil-shaped flashlight out of his coat pocket and swept it slowly around the shabby room. The narrow beam of light showed a couple of armchairs with worn chintz covers, a reproduction of an L.S. Lowry over the mantelpiece, a dining table, the top of which was scratched, and a writing desk. He pulled up a chair and sat down in front of the writing desk and lowered the drop leaf.

The pigeon holes were jammed with old letters, bills, receipts, snapshots, postcards and faded newspaper clippings. Garnett removed the bundle of snapshots and slipped off the elastic band which held them together. They were nearly all black and white, mostly views, but at the bottom of the pile he found two which interested him.

The first showed a young man in dark jeans and check shirt with his arm around the waist of a dark haired girl who leaned against him

20

resting her head on his shoulder. She was wearing ski pants, sweater, and flip flops. There was an ice cream parlour in the background. On the reverse side, written in a round backward sloping hand, were the words, Derek and I—Bournemouth 1968. In the other photograph the girl was alone, dressed in a two piece bathing suit, her arms wrapped about her and a brave smile on her lips. On the back was written, Jean—Blue with cold. He slipped both snapshots into the inside pocket of his coat.

Garnett found that the most recent letters were from friends who dispensed with surnames and addresses and merely signed themselves off as Pauline, Richard, Gwen etc. By checking these with earlier batches, he came up with addresses in the London area which he noted down in his diary. The bills didn't tell him much except that Stanton was frequently short of money and had a hard time making ends meet.

He picked up the newspaper clippings and sorted them out in date order. There seemed to be no apparent reason why Stanton should have bothered to keep them over the years, except that the state of the writing desk was indicative of a man loath to turn anything out. All, except one, were *Telegraph* leaders dealing with the '67 financial crisis. The exception was a short cutting from the *York Evening Press* which gave details of the sudden death of a Mr Arnold Beckwith whilst addressing the Women's Guild. Garnett was about to push it to one side as being of no consequence when he changed his mind and slipped it into his coat pocket.

He closed the desk up, put the chair back in place and went into the bedroom. He checked the contents of the wardrobe, dressing table and chest of drawers, but as far as he could see nothing had been disturbed. He left the bedroom, went back through the lounge and entered the kitchenette. For a moment he thought he heard something, and then he relaxed as he realised that it was merely the occupants of the flat above moving about in their kitchen.

Garnett opened the kitchen door slowly and then slipped across the yard. He unlatched the back gate taking care not to make a noise and stepped out into the alley. He turned to close the gate behind him.

21

A hard, flat voice said; "Hold it."

Garnett glanced out of the corner of his eye. The man was short but compact and his eyes were watchful, alert for the slightest sign of trouble. He was wearing a dark blue raincoat and matching trilby. He held a .38 Police Positive in his right hand, and, from the look on his face, Garnett thought he wouldn't need much encouragement to use it.

The man gestured with the gun. "Face the wall," he said coldly, "Hands above your head, move back a pace and spread your feet." Garnett did as he was told. "That's fine, now lean forward and place your hands against the wall."

The man moved in behind Garnett and jabbed the barrel into his spine. A hand reached inside his pocket and deftly removed his wallet. Stubby fingers explored his body, first down one side and then down the other, probing into every crevice with practised skill. Satisfied that Garnett was clean, the man stepped back a pace and said, harshly, "Name and address?"

"David Garnett, 26 Sutton Square, St Johns Wood."

"Occupation?"

"Debt collector," said Garnett.

"Social Security Card Number?" he barked.

"TX 597840. You'll find everything you want in my wallet."

"I'm asking you. What were you doing in that shop?"

"I wasn't in the shop," Garnett said calmly, "I called on the people in the flat above. They are in arrears."

"You're a liar."

"I'm telling you the truth, you ask them, they'll confirm my story."

"All over town," the man said cynically, "people are beaten up and robbed by men with guns in their hands, but when I take your wallet you make no comment, you assume I'm a policeman. I wonder why?"

"I recognised the big feet."

The man knocked Garnett's hat off, grabbed him by the hair and banged his face against the wall. The blood began to drip from Garnett's nose.

"All right, funny man," he said jerking his head in the direction of the brightly lit street beyond the alley, "let's go and see what the Lieutenant makes of you. Walk in front and keep your hands above your head."

Garnett started to walk slowly towards the lighted street. He gave the impression that he was in a daze, and, stubbing his toe against an uneven flagstone, he tripped and sprawled headlong. Painfully he raised himself up on hands and knees, and shook his head slowly from side to side.

"You clumsy clown," the man said indulgently, "come on, get up."

He got up, felt his ribs gingerly and groaned aloud. As the policeman stepped closer to prod him on his way, Garnett swung round and smashed a rigid forearm into the thick neck, snapping it like a matchstick. The man cannoned back against the wall, fell down on to his knees, and, in slow motion, rolled over on to his right side and lay still.

Garnett bent over the dead man and quickly went through his pockets. He recovered his wallet, picked up the .38 Police Positive and then stood in the shadows while he waited to see if there was a reaction to the noise of the scuffle. When, after a few minutes, nothing had happened, he convinced himself that the policeman had been working alone. Despite the logic of this, when he came to leave the alley, the sweat trickled down his back, his heart thumped madly and the Hillman seemed a hundred kilometres away.

Garnett made the car without incident and thankfully slid inside, hardly daring to believe his luck. He hurriedly wiped the blood off his face with a handkerchief, and then started the car. To his hypersensitive ears the noise of the engine turning over was deafening.

He moved away quickly and dodged through the back streets, trying, unsuccessfully, to work his way back to the main road without passing the front of the arcade. In the process he got himself hopelessly lost in a maze of identical looking streets, ran into a cul de-sac, was forced to reverse and became more confused than ever. Just when he seemed to have lost all sense of direction, he found

23

himself moving along what appeared to be a main road.

In the absence of a better idea, he decided to stay on it and in a short time he came upon a sign which pointed to Oxford in one direction and London in the other, and then he realised that he was on the A40. He began to breathe a little easier.

Ten minutes later, on a quiet stretch of road, he stopped the car, wiped the butt and trigger guard, and then, removing the grating, he dropped the Police Positive down a drain.

He stopped once more before he got back to his flat to mail the diary, the snapshots and the newspaper clipping to Coleman at the office. He marked the envelope personal. It seemed a reasonable precaution.

3

Garnett let himself into the flat, snapped on the light in the sitting room and drew the curtains. He poured himself a whisky and soda and took it into the bedroom where he placed it carefully on the narrow bedside table while he undressed and methodically examined his clothing.

The sleeve of the overcoat had been torn at the elbow and his shirt front was spotted with blood, but apart from a dirt mark on both knees, the suit was not damaged. He cleaned the trousers with Dabitoff, and brushed the suit before putting it away in the wardrobe.

Garnett sat down on the edge of the bed, lit a cigarette, and drank his whisky and soda thoughtfully. The shirt was no problem, he could put it in to soak, and if the stain failed to come out and his daily happened to notice it, he could always claim he had had a nose bleed which was true enough. He had worn chamois leather gloves while he was inside the shop, and wiping the butt and trigger guard of the Police Positive before he dumped it had taken care of any invisible man made fibres which might have been clinging to the weapon. The overcoat would have to go to the invisible menders at the earliest opportunity and that just left the hat.

Leaving the hat behind had been a mistake, not a serious one because, like the rest of his clothes, the maker's name and all other identifying marks had been removed, but a mistake all the same. It was indicative of panic and he liked to think that he was cool and level-headed under pressure.

Garnett drained the whisky, picked up the shirt and went into the bathroom. Putting the shirt in to soak in the wash basin, he stripped off his underclothes and dropped them into the linen basket. He showered, towelled himself vigorously and then examined his damaged nose in the mirror. It was grazed at the tip and slightly swollen but not enough to draw attention to it. He wrapped a bath towel around his waist and padded back to the bedroom.

The telephone shrilled. He answered it and said tersely, "Garnett."

The caller wheezed, cleared his throat and said, "Just rang to see how much longer you would be, David. Everyone else is already here, and Muriel's fussing about the dinner, you know what women are like. I warned her that you might be late."

Garnett recognised the cue and took it up. He said, "I'm afraid the business call took longer than I anticipated but I hope to be with you in about twenty minutes. Please give my apologies to Muriel."

"Not to worry," Coleman said airily. "In a way, your being late is a blessing. I'm running out of sherry—you can never be sure what your guests are going to drink these days. I wonder if you would mind picking up a bottle from the Galleon on your way here?"

"With pleasure," said Garnett.

"Good. See you in another half hour or so."

The phone went dead. Garnett dressed quickly. Fifteen minutes later, he parked the Hillman in the courtyard behind the Galleon and went into the lounge bar.

Someone had taken a great deal of trouble to give the Galleon atmosphere, but when all was said and done it was still a rather seedy and run-down pub littered with bric-a-brac. The walls had been panelled with plywood stained to look like oak; a ship's wheel, a brace of pistols and a rust pitted cutlass were nailed to the beam above the bar, and, as a final touch, the room was poorly lit by clusters of brass coach lanterns.

A few people sat at tables round the room, silent because the piped hi-fi music made normal conversation almost impossible. Two couples occupied all the stools at the bar except one, and they had no difficulty in conversing above the din. Slightly drunk, their inhibitions, if any, had gone by the board. Garnett perched himself on the one vacant stool next to an earthy looking brunette in a mini dress. Endicott was sitting by himself near the entrance to the lounge bar, with an evening paper propped up in front of him and a pint of bitter at his elbow.

Endicott was medium height, stocky, badger grey, and his weather-beaten face and slow speech reminded one of a Dorset farmer, not a superintendent of police. Garnett ordered a Lager and waited for Endicott to make the first move.

In the upside down world in which Garnett lived, the accepted values and moral standards of yesteryear were no longer valid. The uniformed policeman was your enemy because, willingly or not, he maintained law and order for the Puppet Government. The man who robbed a bank to obtain funds for the Resistance was a hero, but if he committed the same act for private gain he was a criminal. The man who shot a traitor in the back was made of sterner stuff than the fireman who rescued a child from a burning building, because his was a continuing risk which was the greater in the long run. The whore who hid a fugitive under the bed while she got laid by a Russian soldier was a better citizen than the woman who kept out of trouble and minded her own business. It was patriotic to deal on the Black Market, to forge petrol coupons and ration books, because in so doing the authority of the Government was undermined.

Judged by these standards, Endicott was neither friend nor enemy. He gathered intelligence and passed it on to the Resistance whose methods he both despised and opposed. In Garnett's opinion, Endicott was the sort who wanted his bread buttered on both sides, and for this reason he did not trust him.

A silken leg brushed against Garnett's and he was aware of the brunette leaning towards him with a bright inviting smile on her face. Her dress was low cut and too tight and he knew he was meant to see the bulge of her milk coloured breasts which were forced up by the type of bra she was wearing.

"Have you got a match?" she asked, and somehow she managed to make even that simple request sound sexy.

Garnett gave her a light from his Ronson. Her kneecap rubbed gently against his thigh. She was sitting with her legs splayed apart so that he should see the white softness of her thighs above the nylons and when she caught him looking the smile became a definite grin.

"Waiting for someone?" she said quietly.

"A friend," said Garnett.

"I'll bet."

Garnett ignored her. He looked at Endicott's reflection in the mirror behind the bar and mentally cursed him for delaying the contact.

The girl had moved closer now and their hips were almost touching. A slim hand with silver fingernails reached out, and, grabbing hold of his glass of lager, threw the contents into Garnett's face.

"You bastard," she shouted, "keep your hands to yourself."

A young, dark man with long sideburns framing a weasel like face appeared at her elbow and pushed Garnett off his stool.

"You dirty old bugger," he snarled, "I saw you shove your hand up her skirt."

Garnett got up off the floor and wiped his face on a handkerchief. "Now look," he said reasonably, "you're making a big mistake."

A short arm jab into the pit of his stomach cut Garnett short. Before he had a chance to cover up, he took a punch in the mouth which split his lip open. Sideburns appeared to be enjoying himself and he moved in to hit Garnett again. It was not a very prudent idea.

Garnett shot out an arm, dug his fingers into the man's windpipe, and, swinging him round, began to batter his head against the imitation oak panelling with the force of a piledriver. For good measure he drew Sideburns forward and kneed him in the groin. The pub suddenly went quiet.

A hand dropped on Garnett's shoulder, and a soft West Country voice said, "All right, that's enough, let him go."

Garnett looked at Endicott and then slowly relaxed his grip.

Endicott said, "I'm a police officer, I want a word with you two outside." He propelled both men out through the door before either had a chance to argue.

The man with sideburns fingered the marks on his throat. "That fugger nearly killed me," he said belligerently.

Endicott looked at him with distaste. "Name and address?" he

28

said disgustedly.

"What for? I didn't start it."

"This man," Endicott said, pointing at Garnett, "assaulted you. I'll need your evidence in court."

"Now look," the man said wheedling, "I don't want to make any trouble. Can't we forget the whole thing? I mean it was just a bit of a lark. It was half my fault anyway." His voice trailed off uncertainly.

Endicott snapped his fingers. "Let's see your Social Security Card," he said and there was a sigh in his voice.

The man reached inside his hip pocket and sullenly produced a dog eared card. Endicott studied it carefully; "Been using this as a toothpick, Cyril?" he enquired.

The man looked down at the pavement and shuffled his feet while Endicott wrote out a receipt and gave it to him.

"I'm going to sleep on this overnight," said Endicott, "maybe I will press charges against you as well, and then maybe again I won't. You can call round to Vine Street Police Station in the morning and collect your card, Mr. Bates. Nine o'clock sharp. Understand?"

Bates nodded.

"All right then, push off before I change my mind and run you in." Endicott touched Garnett on the shoulder, "I'm afraid you are going to have to come with me," he said, "it's a night in the cells for you."

They walked towards the car park. When they were out of earshot, Garnett said, "That was quick thinking but you overplayed your hand."

Endicott grunted; "You've got a nasty temper, you would have killed him if I hadn't stepped between you." Endicott stopped by a black Zodiac, "Get inside," he said.

"What's wrong with my car?"

"You don't seem to understand the situation," Endicott said slowly.

Garnett stared at him in amazement. "You really are going to take me in," he said incredulously.

"Of course I am, I've got to protect myself, a lot of people saw what happened in the bar. You haven't got anything to worry about, I'll see to it that you are let out in the morning."

"What happens to my Hillman in the meantime?"

"I'll get one of my men to take it back to your place."

"All right," said Garnett, "if that's the way you want it."

"It is," said Endicott, "now get inside the car and stop arguing."

As they drove away, Garnett said; "Something's bothering you, why don't you get it off your chest?"

"There are times," said Endicott and there was a bite in his tone, "there are times when I find it difficult to know who the villains really are. When you come right down to fundamentals, you and your sort are merely common murderers and just sitting next to you makes me feel dirty."

"You should take a bath more often."

Endicott pulled up for a traffic light. "That's the kind of smart alec remark I've come to expect of you. One of these days you ought to take a good hard look at what your kind are doing in the name of freedom."

Garnett lit a cigarette, taking care that the filter didn't come into contact with his cut lip. "Some of us," he said quietly, "can't afford the luxury of having a conscience. Four years ago I had a wife, a small son and a house in Keynsham until a SCRAGG Missile with a ten Megaton warhead hit Bristol, and then there was no wife, no son, and no house. Maybe there are people around who can accept the Armistice, but I'm not among their number."

The lights changed to green and they moved forward.

"You're a dedicated hero," Endicott said sarcastically, "you kill in the name of patriotism and enjoy doing it. You ought to see what your handiwork has done to the Swainsons; she's had a nervous breakdown, and her eight year old son can't stop crying because Stanton murdered his father in cold blood. We found Swainson in an ambulance which had been abandoned in Selby Avenue near Queensbury Park Station."

"The sermon's over," said Garnett, "now get down to brass tacks and tell me about Stanton."

"He's probably a killing machine like you, but not as clever. He left a gas pistol behind in Swainson's office together with his briefcase. It was a comparatively simple job to match the prints on the gun against those on the duplicate of his Social Security Card. He is loose but he won't get far, his description will be on the ten o'clock news tonight and in all the papers tomorrow."

Garnett didn't like the sound of that one little bit. The Social Security Card was another name for the Identity card. Two years previously, in an attempt to curb the Resistance, the Government had required every adult over the age of sixteen to register. The card they subsequently issued showed the name, address, description and thumbprint of the holder. The hard core of the Resistance avoided registering and printed their own cards. Why Stanton should have registered and carried an official card was a mystery to Garnett.

Garnett said, "We have to find him before Special Branch does."

"I can understand that," Endicott said dryly. "There was another man in the Swainson's flat. He didn't intend being taken alive; shot the first patrolman in the groin and got the second through the head as he burst through the door. At first we couldn't understand why he hadn't got out with the Stantons and then we found that the kitchen door had been locked on the outside."

"When you use that word, we, I begin to think you've got your loyalties confused."

"I'm not worried what you think, but understand this, I'm not helping you to find Stanton."

Garnett made no reply. He was thinking about Pollard, a man whom he had never met but whose reputation was almost a legend in the Resistance. You thought of Pollard and recalled he had engineered the mass PW escape from Colchester in the early days of the occupation, the destruction of the Vauxhall Bridge Signal Gantry, and, more latterly, the burning of the Antonov 22 fleet at Brize Norton. A man like Pollard was hard to replace and the idea that he was dead left Garnett with a sinking feeling in the pit of his stomach.

"Did you hear what I said?" Endicott asked.

"No," said Garnett.

"I said I wasn't going to play over Stanton."

31

Garnett turned towards him, "Why not?" he said quickly.

"Because I have had enough." Endicott paused and then added, "By God, I have and there are a lot more like me who feel the same way. I didn't like the smell of defeat either, and, like you, I was prepared to do something about it, but after four years I'm beginning to see things differently."

"Are you really," Garnett said in a mocking tone.

A flush began to creep up Endicott's neck. "The trouble with your organisation," he snarled, "is that you don't discriminate enough. In four years you've reduced this country to a state of anarchy where banks are robbed, policemen shot, and innocent men and women are beaten up or murdered in their beds allegedly by the Resistance. Every criminal in the country has been quick to jump on your bandwagon and a lot of decent people are starting to say that the time has come to put a halt to all this. That is why I have finally decided to make the break with you."

"Beginning with Stanton?" Garnett asked mildly.

"You have to draw the line somewhere."

"Now I know you've gone soft in the head." Garnett leaned forward and crushed his cigarette out in the ashtray. "Be honest with yourself for once, you're calling a halt because you've got the wind up."

"The hell with you," Endicott said wearily. He swung the car off the main road into the Station Yard. "Vine Street," he said heavily, "your board and lodging for the night. The beds are reasonable but we only serve a light breakfast."

Chief Inspector Williamson was a sad faced looking man in his late fifties who had run to fat. He had long since reached his ceiling in the police force, and this, so Garnett thought, would account for his sad face. He looked tired and bad tempered and he chewed continuously on the stem of his pipe.

His eyes lit up momentarily when he saw Endicott and he extended a podgy hand in greeting. "Good to see you, Dick," he said.

Endicott shook his head warmly, "And you, Arthur, we should get together more often. How's the wife?"

32

"Doris is keeping well." He waved a hand, "Sit down, Dick, make yourself comfortable. How's Mary?"

Endicott lowered his bulk into the chair. "She's fine," he said, "gets a bit depressed now and then, it's the change of life you know."

Williamson sucked on his pipe. "We're none of us getting any younger, Dick. I'm thinking of retiring, got my eye on a semi-detached down Farnborough way."

"Funny you should think of going too. Mary's been on to me about packing it in, wants to go back to Bridport."

"We went to Lyme Regis for a holiday once; I rather liked it and toyed with the idea of living down there when we retired but we are town birds at heart." Williamson smiled, "Anyway," he said, "you obviously didn't come here just for a chit chat, what can I do for you, Dick?"

Endicott reached inside his coat and laid a dog eared card on Williamson's desk. "A man called Cyril Bates will come round for this tomorrow morning at nine o'clock. I'd like you to read him the riot act about behaving himself in the future and then let him go. Tell him we're not pressing charges this time."

"Is that all?"

"No, I want this other man locked up for the night. Book him for drunk and disorderly and then wheel him up before the magistrate in the morning. I'll let you have a statement."

Williamson said, "I'll go and get a shorthand writer, the damn intercom is on the blink again." He looked at Garnett and said, "You're allowed to make one call."

Garnett reached for the phone, but Williamson brushed his hand away, "Just give me the number," he said, "and I'll get it for you."

Garnett shoved his hands in his pockets and remained silent.

"Ah," Endicott said in disgust, "let him make the call, Arthur, if it makes him any the happier."

Williamson pushed the phone across the desk. Garnett picked it up and rang Coleman's number.

"Hugh?" said Garnett, "this is David. I'm afraid I won't be able to make dinner after all. I ran into a little trouble at the Galleon and

I've been picked up and charged with being drunk and disorderly." He paused and then said, "No, I don't think that will be necessary, Superintendent Endicott has assured me that it will come to nothing. I'm sorry about dinner; please apologise to Muriel again for me."

He hung up and smiled at Endicott. Williamson got to this feet and strolled over to the door. He looked back at Garnett and said to Endicott, "You've got a cocky one there, Dick, a month inside would do him the world of good." He went out closing the door behind him.

Endicott said, "That was a damn fool thing to do."

"I don't think so," said Garnett, "now you know that if anything should happen to me, someone is going to come looking for you, and instead of a cottage in Bridport you'll retire to a cemetery."

4

As he went through the entrance to Crescent House, Garnett caught a final glimpse of his watch dog reflected in the glass door, and for a brief moment he was tempted to turn round and give him a farewell salute, but on reflection he saw little point in making the gesture.

The man had not attempted to make himself inconspicuous from the moment he had picked Garnett up outside the Magistrates' Court, nor when he had subsequently followed him back to the flat, and then, just as doggedly, shadowed him all the way back to the office. It only made sense to Garnett on the assumption that either Endicott wanted him to know that he was being followed, or, alternatively, he was there to distract attention from someone else.

Garnett was feeling rough. An uncomfortable night in the cells with two drunks who had vomited over him, followed by an appearance before a magistrate who had imposed a twenty pound fine was not the best way to start the day.

He took the lift up to the fourth floor and found Dane waiting for him in the office. She was wearing a pale blue cotton tunic cut in the Cossack style, her blonde hair was done up in a switch, and in high heeled shoes there wasn't much difference in their respective heights. There were times when she seemed to be distant. This was one of them; she had that cool, detached, faraway, mysterious look which the Swedish women seem to go in for when they run out of ideas.

"Mr Coleman wants to see you in his office immediately," she said coolly.

"I'm not surprised," said Garnett.

"In that case, why not try getting to the office on time?"

He stared at her, and then said, "Aren't you forgetting yourself?"

35

"One of these days I might just do that," she said in a level voice.

"And what's that supposed to mean?"

"Whatever you choose to make of it."

"Oh, for God's sake," he said irritably, "if there is one thing I can't stand, it's a woman who talks in riddles. Why don't you say what you're thinking."

"All right," she snapped, the colour mounting in her face, "I think you're bloody rude and insufferable." She walked out of the room, slamming the door behind her.

Aloud, Garnett said, "I wonder what the hell's got into that woman." Unable to think of a reason for the outburst, he shrugged his shoulders, hung his coat up on the rack and then went along to Coleman's office.

Coleman looked calm enough but Garnett could read the danger signals. The green inhaler was working overtime, and when Coleman was angry his asthma got progressively worse. He flopped into a chair and waited for Coleman to say his piece. He didn't have long to wait.

"I congratulate you," Coleman said heavily. "At least you had the foresight to post the results of your burglary on to me before you elected to spend the night in gaol."

"It wasn't from choice."

"Jesus Christ," Coleman shouted, "I didn't suppose it was. I want to hear your explanation."

"Endicott had me set up for it."

"It was a sudden flare up and you lost your temper." Coleman's face was the colour of puce. He reached for his inhaler and took a couple of whiffs.

Garnett said; "One of these days you're going to drop dead."

"We'll leave my state of health out of it. Get back to the point."

"The point is Endicott delayed making contact with me, and there's only one explanation for that. He knew there was going to be trouble and he wanted a legitimate excuse to have me arrested."

"Now I've heard everything," Coleman said sarcastically.

"You haven't heard anything yet. Endicott wants out. He pitched me a sob story to the effect that after four years a lot of decent

36

people had had enough of violence. They think we're little better than common criminals. He said we are losing support all along the line."

"He could be right."

"Suppose he is. What's the alternative? To stop fighting?"

"Perhaps we should adjust to the situation. Learn to live with the Russians and gradually absorb them into our way of life. A sort of passive resistance to preserve our heritage as best we can. It's been done before."

"Like the ancient Britons and the Romans?"

"Precisely," said Coleman.

"Or the Saxons and the Normans," suggested Garnett, "only in their case I wonder who absorbed who." Garnett leaned forward in his chair. "Four years ago," he said, "we lost a battle, not a war. The only way we'll ever get the Russians off our backs is to make this island a barren and inhospitable place and we should be prepared to fight for five, ten, twenty, fifty or even a hundred years if necessary. Anyway, Endicott was just looking for an excuse. He's got the wind up, and he is using me as a lever to get out of the Resistance."

"Go on," said Coleman, "I'm interested."

"You know the routine when you're arrested. These days you're mugged and fingerprinted before you're even convicted. So there's the threat. When he decides to run a check on my prints—"

"He will know you are an ex con with quite a record."

"I wouldn't put it quite like that."

"All right, you're an escaped PW. I wonder if Endicott knows for certain who your control is?"

"I've got a tail and a rather obvious one at that. I think Endicott already knows you're my control. The tail is there to throw a scare into you."

"Since you chose to call me when you got into trouble last night," Coleman said icily, "and as you have led your shadow straight to this building, I have no doubt that he does have a pretty shrewd idea, but having a shrewd idea and being certain are two different matters. What do you think his next move will be?"

"When he is sure, he's going to make a deal with you. The deal is

37

you stop pressing him for information which he considers is too risky, and in return he lets me off the hook. No check will be run on my record and your department is safe."

"You killed an agent from Special Branch last night," Coleman said, changing the subject.

"It couldn't be avoided."

"I take it you didn't leave your fingerprints all over the bookshop?"

"I wore gloves."

"Anything to connect you with the dead man?"

"Not a thing."

"Thank God for small mercies," Coleman said dryly. "Nonetheless you're becoming hot."

"Does that mean you plan to rest me?"

"I don't know. Perhaps."

"What about the Stantons?"

"A check is already being made on the addresses listed in your diary."

"Including York?"

"Of course. I assumed the newspaper cutting about Arnold Beckwith was supposed to have some significance."

"So what do I do now?"

"Try earning your pay as a solicitor," said Coleman.

"You haven't asked me about Pollard."

"What about him?" said Coleman.

"He's dead."

"So I assumed."

"You don't seem surprised."

"You're not the only horse in my stable," Coleman said quietly.

Garnett went back to his office. He found that a dark haired girl from the typing pool had replaced Dane who had been taken sick, or so the replacement said. The rest of the morning passed slowly.

At one o'clock Garnett left the building, and, accompanied by his persistent watch dog, had a dreary lunch in the Quick Eats Snack Bar. He ate a couple of tasteless meat sandwiches washed down with a cup of lukewarm coffee sweetened with saccharine. Finding that he still had an hour to kill, Garnett drifted into a News Theatre. He came in at the tail end of the newsreel in time to see the closing seconds of the match between Red Army and Chelsea, which the Pensioners lost four two. The result seemed to please the commentator. An old Donald Duck film failed to amuse him and the documentary showing the rebuilding of Bristol so sickened him that he left the cinema before it ended.

He got back to the office at two-fifteen, went through the in tray and dictated a few letters. He was reading *The Times* leader when the West Indian was shown into his office.

"My name's Robinson," the man said, smiling, "okay if I came in?"

He was about five foot six, broad shouldered and narrow hipped. He walked on the balls of his feet and moved quickly and silently. That, and a lump of scar tissue over his right eye, added up to a prize fighter. He wore a crumpled brown pin stripe and carried a shabby mac. Garnett thought he probably wasn't making very much out of the game.

He sat down in a chair facing Garnett. "I have a problem," he said.

Garnett tossed *The Times* into the out tray and leaned back in his chair. "Most of my clients have."

"I think you would call my problem a matter of race relations."

Garnett's smile faded. "I'm afraid that sort of thing is rather out of our field; we specialise in conveyancing. The police normally handle all prosecutions under the Race Relations Act. I think you would be better advised to put your problem to them."

Robinson smiled thinly. "You're a solicitor aren't you? I mean I am at liberty to consult you, right?"

Garnett nodded in agreement.

"Okay. Now I come down here from Birmingham because a friend offered me a better paid job but I had no place to live. I see some adverts in the evening paper which seem right for me; so today I go calling to find me a room. First I go to see a Mrs Richard Westbury of 33 Tonbridge Vale over in Peckham."

Robinson paused and Garnett found himself listening with

39

interest.

"Then I call on a Miss Gwen Heath at 259 Hanger Lane, Ealing, and finally I get around to a Mrs Keith Parker, 16 Trentham Gardens, Hammersmith; and you know what, man? Not one of these good people have a room to let. You think I've got a case?"

Garnett smiled. "Did you have the same sort of trouble in York?" he asked.

Robinson looked puzzled. "I haven't been to York, Mr Garnett. I had no call to, I want to live in this town." He reached inside his brown pin stripe jacket and placed a card on Garnett's desk. "You think about what I told you, Mr Garnett," he said, "you can find me at this address any time."

He stood up and walked towards the door. "I don't hold with folk telling me lies, man, they shouldn't put it in the paper if they don't want to rent me a room." He looked back at Garnett and winked. "It's no laughing matter, man," he said solemnly. He went out and closed the door behind him.

Garnett reached for the intercom and called Coleman. He heard Coleman wheezing heavily before he answered.

Garnett said; "I looked into the conveyancing of those three properties which interested you and I can see no reason why there should be a delay. Everything is perfectly straightforward and above board."

Coleman said; Thank you, I thought it would be." The intercom went dead.

Garnett picked up the card Robinson had left on his desk. The printing on the front said, Harry's Revue Bar and underneath was the legend. Make a date with us tonite. The word tonite had been underlined in ink. He slipped the card into his wallet and left the office.

Garnett let himself into the flat, switched on the light and drew the curtains. His watch dog, bored and not a little cold, was leaning against the railings on the opposite side of the street looking up at the flat. Like the poor, it seemed he was always going to be around.

He wondered how far Endicott was prepared to go. On impulse he picked up the phone, listened carefully and then dialled TIM. The talking clock informed him that at the third stroke it would be six twenty-three precisely. He replaced the phone thoughtfully; the knowledge that it was bugged didn't make him feel any too happy.

Garnett went into the kitchen and made himself a cup of tea and, switching on the National transistor, settled down to read the *Evening News* against a background noise of pop music. The lead story still dealt with Blythe's assassination. There was now a thirty thousand pound reward for information leading to Stanton's arrest but still no picture of him. Despite the hazy description, he didn't give Stanton much chance. He saw that Harrow was still under strict curfew and the Government had slapped a collective fine of half a million on the borough, which was a novel way of collecting revenue even if it didn't make them many friends. The editorial seemed to approve of the Government's action, but papers had to print pretty much what the Government wanted them to say these days.

He pushed the paper to one side and finished his tea. If Stanton's chances were poor, his own position was far from healthy. Coleman was very good at protecting his own skin, making quite sure that people like Endicott never met him face to face, but now of course all that was changed. Endicott could use Garnett to get at Coleman. He wondered how long it would be before Coleman gave him the sack. A cold shudder ran down his spine. Suppose his watch dog wasn't a policeman? Suppose it was Coleman who was having him followed as a form of insurance in case he became too hot?

Garnett went through his wallet and took out Robinson's calling card and examined it again. He had no doubt whatever that he was expected to call at Harry's Revue and this simple hunch was a comfort. For the time being at least, he had no worries about the future.

In defeat, every Capital City spawns a thousand gay night haunts to suit every jaded taste. They seem to mushroom overnight and disappear into oblivion just as quickly. Harry's Revue Bar was a cut above most as far as the fittings and the drink went, but it still had its quota of beautiful women with prominent collar bones and genitals under the long gowns, and boyish looking young men who

41

were women, and straightforward queers and lesbians among its members. Harry's Revue Bar also had a degree of permanence which was more than most of the night spots had.

The floor show was still in progress when Garnett arrived. A blonde, dressed in a strapless black sheath which looked as though it had been resurrected from the early sixties, glided between the crowded tables crooning softly into a hand mike. "Long ago and far away," she sang and the nostalgic sentiment got through to the audience, reminded them of a more carefree world and they loved her for it.

Garnett found a place at the bar and ordered a whisky and soda. The blonde gave way to a couple of dark haired girls in leather suits and kinky boots. The lights went down and a small spot picked them out on the stage. The girls looked bored with the routine but the audience clearly wasn't. As they stripped each other in slow time, the press at the bar thinned out considerably.

Garnett finished his drink and ordered another. Through the haze, he could see his watch dog seated at a table near the door, nursing what appeared to be a soft drink. The man was probably no more than twenty-three or -four but his receding mouse coloured hair made him look older at first sight. He was, Garnett thought, a detective constable possibly new to the job and wondering what the hell he was supposed to be doing. Maybe Endicott had omitted to tell him. In any event the bare buttocks of the show girls interested him more than Garnett did at the moment.

The lights went up, the girls strutted off the stage to frantic applause and the crowd began to drift back to the bar.

A hand struck Garnett on the shoulder and the drink in his hand slopped over his shirt and jacket. A fair haired young man said; "I'm so sorry, how frightfully clumsy of me."

"It's nothing," said Garnett.

"Oh, but it is, I've made you spill your drink all over your suit." He pulled a handkerchief out of his pocket and sponged the lapels of Garnett's suit.

The girl who was with him said, "George, do be careful, let me take your glass before you spill another lot over the poor man." She turned to Garnett and said, brightly, "I'm afraid George has had too much to drink, you know how it is."

The man had his hand inside Garnett's jacket. He swayed slightly on his feet and his breath smelt of drink but not enough to convince Garnett that he wasn't acting the part. If he was a dip, he had lost his touch.

He stood back and smiled vacantly at Garnett. "There, old chap," he said in his condescending voice, "doesn't look too bad now."

"You can buy me a drink," said Garnett.

The man hesitated, and then collecting his wits, said, "Of course, what'll you have, old boy?"

"Whisky soda." Garnett smiled at the girl, "My name's David Garnett," he said.

"I'm Gillian Worsley." She faltered, "And this is my husband, George."

"Do you live near here?"

"Quite close," she said

"Don't dry up on me," Garnett said quietly. "I'm afraid we have to make small talk. I'm being watched, and your hushand has just planted something on me. I know you want to get out of here, but this has to look absolutely right. I could be picked up and searched within minutes of leaving if they think anything funny is going on."

"As a matter of fact," Gillian said brightly, "we have a flat in South Kensington."

"You were lucky to find one there; I thought most of the available accommodation thereabouts had been swallowed up by the Russian Control Commission?"

"Well, that's quite true, but you see we were given priority because George works for them."

Worsley said, "Your drink, old man." He raised his glass and said, "Cheers."

Gillian said, "I've just been telling Mr Garnett that you work for the Control Commission, George."

"Oh, yes?" he said vaguely. "I'm an accountant, you know, working in their Reparations Section. They mean to bleed us white."

"Did you expect anything else? After all they won the war."

43

"So they keep telling me," Worsley said gloomily. "They mean to turn us into a nation of farmers."

"Sounds like Morgenthau," said Garnett.

"Who's he?"

"An American. He had much the same thing in mind for Germany after the Second World War."

Worsley tossed his drink back. "Trust them to lift someone else's plan. A car for every Russian made in Birmingham. They'll have all of us walking before long. My car's been off the road for three weeks waiting for two new tyres, and I'm supposed to have priority. It makes me so angry when I think that a few years ago I traded my car in for a new one every twelve months."

"Most of us have taken a knock one way or the other," Garnett said mildly.

"My goodness, yes," Gillian said morosely, "when I think of what poor daddy has had to put up with. He had to sell our lovely house at Goring you know; couldn't afford to keep it up once they closed the Stock Exchange. The Government bought it at a ridiculously low price. I mean the house not the Stock Exchange."

"Gillian was a Crispin-Blousefield before we were married," Worsley said owlishly.

Garnett had never heard of the Crispin-Blousefields but he looked suitably impressed.

"Well, of course that isn't strictly true," Gillian said, "I was married to a dreadful little man in the FO before I met George."

"But you were a Crispin-Blousefield, darling," Worsley protested.

"Oh, indeed yes. I came out in '67, wonderful season despite Mr Wilson." She smiled brightly at Garnett, "You can't imagine what it was like—the super dances and parties; heavenly, how I miss it all now."

"Would you like to dance?"

"Love to," she said without enthusiasm. She handed her bag to Worsley. "Look after this, darling," she said, "I shan't be long."

Garnett steered her on to the floor. She was distant, wooden faced and hoping she wouldn't have to spend more than a few minutes with him. She kept him at arm's length as though he was a bad smell

44

and her gaze was directed at a point above his right shoulder. Her attitude suggested they had nothing in common and Garnett wouldn't quarrel with that assumption. They were both relieved when the band stopped playing.

Garnett walked her back to the bar, said goodnight to them both and collected his raincoat from the cloakroom.

The snow, which had been threatening to appear all day, was falling lightly. He turned his coat collar up and stepped out into the street; old faithful dogged his heels at a discreet distance.

When he got back to the flat, Garnett made himself a cup of instant coffee, and sat down in the kitchen to examine the contents of the envelope which Worsley had planted on him. There was a letter from the Cavendish Hotel in York confirming a Mr Daniel's reservation, a Social Security card in the same name and a return train ticket.

It seemed Stanton hadn't made a very good job of covering his tracks and he wasn't sure whether that was a good omen or not.

5

Garnett reached out an arm and stopped the jangling alarm clock. He stretched his arms above his head, yawned, and, fighting back the desire to nestle down again into the comfort of the warm bed, flung the blankets aside.

Shivering in the cold, he went to the window and carefully drew the curtain back a fraction. The half light of dawn distorted the familiar shapes and played tricks with the senses, but as his eyes gradually became accustomed to the light, he saw that his tail had been changed. The new man was shorter.

A thin blanket of snow covered the street. The detective, apparently tired of stamping up and down the pavement to keep warm, moved back to shelter in the doorway of the house opposite, and only the telltale glow of a cigarette now betrayed his presence. Garnett allowed the curtain to fall back in place.

He switched the table lamp on, put on a dressing gown and sat down on the bed. He was faced with three problems; getting rid of the woman who came in to clean the flat up every morning around nine, warning Coleman that the phone was tapped, and shaking off his tail. It occurred to Garnett that he was going to need some help.

He got up and went into the bathroom. Opening the medicine cabinet he found a box of yellow pills, deliberated how many he should take and finally decided to make it two. He washed them down with a glass of tepid water.

The Lab technicians claimed that the pills were guaranteed to produce very quick results. They were absolutely right. Less than five minutes later beads of sweat began to collect on his forehead and his stomach began to churn. His body felt as if it was on fire and there was a gagging sensation at the back of his throat which he

46

could not contain. Garnett leaned forward and vomited repeatedly into the basin.

Feeling weak and exhausted, he staggered back into the bedroom, dropped his dressing gown on to the floor and fell into bed. The ceiling whirled above him and he drifted off into a restless sleep.

He awoke to heavy footsteps in the lounge. The bedroom door opened inwards and Mrs Samson poked her head inside. The inevitable cigarette was stuck in the corner of her mouth and the drifting smoke made her squint.

She surveyed him calmly and then said, "You don't look very well, Mr Garnett. What's the matter with you?"

"I've been sick, I think I've picked up a bug or something."

She seemed disappointed that his complaint wasn't more serious. "Sent for the doctor, have you?" she said listlessly.

"I don't think that will be necessary. I'll be all right in a day or two." A lump of ash parted company from the cigarette and was deftly trodden into the carpet. Her birdlike eyes darted about the room and then came to rest at a point on the wall above his head as the idea took root in her mind.

"I always say bed's the best place to be when you're out of sorts," she said philosophically. "That and peace and quiet. I expect you would like me to give the flat a quick flick over with the duster and then leave you in peace?"

"If you wouldn't mind."

She brightened visibly. "Of course I don't mind, you don't want me banging and crashing about the place when you're feeling off colour. Tell you what, I'll make you a cup of tea before I go."

"I am afraid the bathroom is in a bit of a mess. I've been sick."

"Don't you worry about that, Mr. Garnett. I'll soon clear it up."

For a small woman she made plenty of noise. Garnett wondered if this was deliberate in case he should change his mind; if she but knew it, there was no chance of that.

She was as good as her word. The flat literally did get a quick going over with a duster, and the cup of tea, which she placed on the bedside table before she left, had the look and consistency of Brown Windsor soup. He declined to drink it, not that it hurt her feelings;

47

she had already left, banging the door behind her.

Garnett waited a few minutes, and then, sitting up in bed, rang Coleman at the office. He placed a handkerchief over the mouthpiece and said, "Hugh? This is David. I should have called you before now, but I'm afraid I was feeling too sick."

"There's nothing wrong, is there?"

"Only with this telephone, I can scarcely hear you. Can you hear me?"

Coleman got the message. "It must be a bad connection. I'm told that's a fault with party lines."

"I haven't got a party line, but that's beside the point. I think I've picked up a bug, anyway I feel pretty sick. I had to send my daily home and it looks as though I will have to spend a day or two in bed. The prospect of being cooped up in this flat appals me."

"You don't sound at all well to me. I think you ought to stay in bed. Forget about the office, we can handle things this end."

Garnett said; "Thank you for being so considerate." He hung up, got out of bed and moved to the window where he could watch his shadow.

The watery sun clouded over and the first raindrop splattered against the window and traced a meandering path down the length of the pane. The steady drizzle persisted and slowly turned the thin layer of snow into slush. A van moved up the quiet street, its tyres hissing on the wet tarmac.

The detective, his raincoat collar turned up, was leaning against the telephone box at the end of the street. Presently he went inside the box and picked up the phone. He spoke to someone for a few seconds and then came out again, looked up at Garnett's flat and shrugged his shoulders.

Garnett moved back out of sight. He had seen enough to know that his conversation with Coleman had been monitored and passed across as he had hoped it would. There was a chance that from now on the detective would lose interest and would not be as observant.

Garnett washed, shaved, and pulled on a pair of slacks and a sweater. He packed his shaving kit, pair of pyjamas, shirt, socks, tie, suit and mac in a small grip and then went into the kitchen, where

48

he made himself a cup of coffee and toasted a couple of slices of bread.

Time passed slowly. An hour, then two, then three passed. Lunch came and went, and still no move by Coleman. The waiting began to get him down. It always did. He remembered the time he had gone over the wall at Lichfield. He'd waited in the shadows for God knows how long, watching the searchlights and calculating how long the spot he had chosen to go over would be in darkness. His legs had trembled like a racehorse under starter's orders and he wanted to urinate. When, finally, he decided it was time to go, his legs seemed rooted to the spot.

The front door bell brought Garnett back to the present and he moved quickly to see who it was.

The man was wearing a dun coloured knee length smock and was carrying a laundry box under each arm. He was about Garnett's height and build but mousy, thin faced, sallow, and as sharp and fly as a barrow boy.

"The name's Baker," he said, as he shouldered past Garnett. "Close the door, we've got exactly four minutes."

Garnett said; "All right, tell me what to do."

Baker dropped the laundry boxes and slipped out of the smock. "Get into this," he said, "it looks as though you are going to need my pants as well."

"Do you do this often?"

"We can skip the jokes, friend. The laundry van is parked outside the block, driver's seat nearest the kerb. You are to leave the van in the back yard of the Express Laundry Service Depot in Grafton Street. You can change your clothing in the office. They're expecting you."

Garnett changed slacks and zipped up the fly. "Anything else I should know?" he said.

"We've set up a pattern of callers on the block; door to door Fuller Brush man, Interflora delivered early daffodils to the woman downstairs, she was rather surprised about that."

"I'll bet she was, she doesn't know a soul."

"Yes? Well, it's made her day then. In another couple of minutes,

49

a white Morris 1000 is going to pull up opposite your watchdog. The driver will keep him talking while you slip into the van. Keys are in the dashboard, brakes have a tendency to fade, and watch it when you start her up, she has a habit of flooding."

"You sound like a second hand car dealer."

Baker eyed him coldly. "You'd better get moving, hadn't you?"

Garnett picked up one of the laundry boxes and took it into the bedroom.

Baker said, "Now what the hell?"

"I'm going to pack my grip inside the box. Any objections?"

"Not if you get a move on," said Baker.

Garnett returned carrying one laundry box, picked up the other and said, "Help yourself to a drink. Don't answer the telephone, it's bugged." He opened the door and left Baker to close it behind him.

Garnett walked downstairs and kept out of sight in the hall until he heard a car pull up, its brakes squealing. A loud voice said, "Am I all right for Eltham Crescent?"

Garnett slipped out through the doors into the street. He put the laundry boxes into the back of the van keeping his face averted, and closed the sliding doors. He moved unhurriedly although the desire was to do otherwise. Sliding into the driver's seat, he switched on the ignition and pressed the starter. The engine turned over laboriously and it took all of his skill and coolness to nurse it into life. He checked the road in the rear view mirror before he pulled out. The detective wasn't even looking in his direction.

A quarter of an hour later, Garnett swung into the yard of the Express Laundry Service Depot and parked the van alongside the loading bay. An old man poked his head out of the checkers' office and beckoned him to come inside. Garnett jumped out of the cab, collected the laundry box containing his clothes and walked quickly up the short flight of steps leading to the checkers' office.

The old man held the door open for him. "Nasty weather we've been having today," he said cheerfully.

"It could be worse."

"It could at that." He lifted a blackened pot off the coke stove. "Care for a cup of tea?"

"No thanks. Is it all right if I change here?"

"Go ahead, don't mind me."

The old man slopped the brown liquid into a chipped enamel mug and drank from it noisily. He smacked his lips appreciatively. "Good cup that," he said, "puts wool in your socks." He nodded towards the desk. "That briefcase is for you. Gent said you'd pick it up. That's a nice suit you've got there, mate, bet it set you back a pretty penny."

"Sixty quid."

The man whistled. "All right for some."

"It's an investment, it'll last me for years."

"It'd need to at that price."

"How do I get out of here?"

"Same way as you came in, through the back yard."

Garnett pressed a pound note into his outstretched hand. "That's for the use of your office."

"You're welcome, mate, don't forget your briefcase. I'll see to the van."

Garnett left the office, dodged through the yard carefully, avoiding the puddles, and hopped a bus in the high street. He got off at Chalk Farm, took the tube to Tottenham Court Road, switched to the Central for Liverpool Street and then cut back to King's Cross on the Circle line. He caught the four thirty-eight stopping train to York and had a compartment to himself.

There was a copy of the *Daily Mirror* on the seat opposite which caught his eye. The headline above the picture read, Have you seen this couple?

They were standing outside a Registry Office. The man wore a white carnation in his buttonhole and the girl was in a mini dress. He wondered how he had come to overlook that particular photograph when he went through the Stantons' flat.

6

The train was running seventy-eight minutes behind time when it eventually arrived in York. Garnett walked across the wooden passenger bridge and surrendered his ticket to the collector at the gate on Platform One. In an otherwise empty arcade, the two men lounging by Smith's bookstall stood out a mile.

The taller of the two was wearing a long black overcoat which reached below the knees, and his thin, sad looking face would have done credit to an undertaker. The shorter man was just under six foot, wore a hip length suede and sheepskin jacket and was much younger than his companion. Garnett thought he was about twenty-six and probably wore his yellow hair short because he fancied it made him look a hard man. They had police written all over them.

As he came into the main hall, the young one stepped forward and caught hold of his arm. He flashed a card under Garnett's nose; "Markham," he said, "Yorkshire Police, City Division. Let's see your Social Security Card?"

Garnett dropped the grip and reached inside his breast pocket. He was aware that Markham's companion had sidled up behind him, and instinctively the other passengers were giving them a wide berth. He handed the card to Markham who scanned it quickly.

"What brings you to York, Mr Daniel?"

Garnett patted the briefcase under his arm. "Insurance business, I'm with the Axel Group."

"How long are you planning to stay?"

"Two, maybe three days; depends on how things go."

Markham held out his hand. "We'll just take a look in that briefcase of yours, Mr Daniel." He nodded at his companion and said, "You'd better make sure he is clean, Jack."

A voice behind Garnett said; "We get all kinds of weirdies these days. Raise your hands above your head, Mr Daniel."

Markham smiled thinly. "It's just routine, you understand, nothing personal. We like a quiet life in these parts, keeps the Russians out of our hair. Been with the Axel group long?"

"Just over two years."

"Don't hold with insurance myself but the old lady swore by your lot, they helped to bury me Dad. I see you're staying at the Cavendish—nice hotel—quiet but nice."

Garnett said, "Is it okay if I lower my arms now?"

"As long as Jack is happy."

"I'm never happy."

Garnett could understand that. If the man had smiled his face might have cracked in half.

"He's got a dry sense of humour has our Jack Halliday, Mr Daniel." Markham held out the briefcase. "All right," he said, "you can go."

"Thank you."

"You won't find any taxis in the yard at this time of night. You'll have to take a bus up to the Avenue. The Cavendish is about a kilometer beyond St Peter's School on your right opposite the village green."

"Thank you," said Garnett for the second time.

Markham held up the Social Security Card. "Don't forget this, Mr Daniel, you won't get very far without it."

"I'll be forgetting my own head next."

"Can you make that a promise," Halliday growled.

Markham's face creased with mirth. "I told you he had a rare sense of humour," he said.

The bus was empty except for two Russian soldiers sitting up front. They wore olive drab greatcoats and the mauve coloured shoulder boards of the mechanised infantry. They sat rigidly to attention, eyes staring ahead, and ignored Garnett. They were still sitting there like switched off robots when he left the bus.

It was a crisp night and there were odd patches of snow still lying

53

about which had survived the thaw. The streets were deserted and most of the houses were in darkness. Bed was the warmest place to be on a cold night when there was a fuel crisis, and there had been such a crisis every winter since the occupation began.

The Cavendish was a small hotel situated at the far end of Earswick Road and was the only place in the street which showed any sign of life. Garnett wondered what had become of the people who used to live in the other tall, solid, Victorian houses on either side of the Cavendish, which now stood empty and forlorn. The hotel boasted an oak nail studded door and mock coach lamps. He pushed the door open and went inside.

The hall was carpeted from wall to wall. Glassy eyed moth eaten deer heads looked down on him from the dark stained panels on the wall above his head. Generations of spiders had weaved an intricate pattern of cobwebs in the decaying antlers. Garnett walked up to the reception desk and rang the bell for attention.

Prominently displayed, as the emergency laws decreed, was a list of wanted men. Top of the list was John Richard Seymour alias John Evans alias Richard Pollard. Next in line was Janet Prentice, a dark woman with short black hair who had organised the first underground newspaper before becoming the head of Intelligence for South-East England. Garnett knew for a fact that she had died of pneumonia some eighteen months previously. Her presence on the list was a positive reminder that the enemy's Intelligence system was far from being infallible.

Garnett rang the bell a second time. A bald headed man emerged through a door marked private and eyed him coldly.

Garnett said, "I'm Mr Daniel, I believe you have a room for me?"

The man pushed the hotel register across the desk with one hand while reaching for a key on the board behind him with the other. "Room number eleven," he said. "Will you be staying long?"

Garnett looked up. "A couple of days at the most."

The man sucked on his teeth noisily. "Aye, well, if you should stay longer than that, I'll want a ration card from you."

"I'll bear that in mind, Mr ?"

"Hunt."

"Thank you."

"Dinner finishes in another quarter of an hour."

"That's all right, I had a bowl of soup on the train."

Hunt snapped his fingers—"Nearly forgot." He reached under the counter and placed a small box in front of Garnett. "These are the cigars you ordered from Harrisons'," he said.

Garnett looked at the box thoughtfully. "I'm glad they managed to meet my request," he said. He wedged the box under his arm.

"Can you manage everything?"

"I think so."

"We're short of staff, you see," said Hunt.

"It's the same wherever you go, everything's self service these days."

Garnett slipped the key to the room into his pocket, picked up the briefcase in one hand and the grip in the other, and went upstairs. He unlocked the door of his room, switched on the light, and dumped his things on to the bed. Closing the door, he removed his mac and then sat down in the wicker armchair.

The cigar box was heavier than it should have been. He tore the wrapping paper off and prised open the lid. The Remington Rand .45 Automatic, cased in a black leather shoulder holster, nestled coyly on a bed of cotton wool surrounded by seven soft nosed bullets.

Picking up the shells, he fed them into the magazine which he then slapped into the butt. He snapped the action back, feeding a round up into the chamber, eased the hammer forward under control, and put the change lever to safe.

Garnett slotted the gun into the holster and then placed it under the pillow. The Remington was a precision made job, impressive, but a gun with too much stopping power for what he had in mind. Given the choice, he would have preferred something a little more discreet, around a .32 calibre, but guns were not all that easy to come by, and you had to use what you were given.

Garnett unpacked the grip, hung the clothes up in the wardrobe and laid his shaving gear out on the glass shelf above the wash basin. He was just rinsing his hands and face when someone tapped on the door and came into the room. Looking up, he saw Dane's reflection in the mirror.

She stopped dead, her jaw dropped and there were no prizes for guessing that Dane was equally surprised to see him. Recovering her presence of mind, she closed the door behind her.

Garnett dried his hands and face, hung the towel back on the rail and turned to face her. "I'm glad to see you've recovered so quickly," he said blandly.

She compressed her lips and there was an angry glint in her eyes, and he knew that some tart remark would come tumbling out. He wasn't disappointed.

"You have a schoolboy sense of humour."

"I wasn't trying to be funny."

"You succeeded then; you weren't."

"Now who's being rude and insufferable?"

"I am," she said grimly. "I've taken a leaf out of your book."

"All right; so you'd love to scratch my eyes out, maybe you'll get a chance. Are you staying here?"

"In the adjoining room."

"How convenient."

She ignored him. She sat down on the bed, opened her handbag and rummaged through the contents. It was one of those giant sized bags which women seem to like because it saves having a vanity case and they can also carry their life history around with them. It took her some seconds to locate the street plan of York. She unfolded the map and laid it out on the bed and motioned Garnett to look over her shoulder.

"They're staying at 49 Tolcroft Road," she said, pointing to the map. "As you can see, it's a cul-de-sac off the A19 which runs down to the Ouse. Mrs Arnold Beckwith owns the house, she takes in lodgers."

"Are you sure they are there?"

"Positive."

"How?"

"Because I have seen them."

Garnett pulled on the lobe of his right ear. "Do you mind

56

enlarging on that?" he said.

"A telex was sent to Mr Hunt asking him to locate a Mrs Arnold Beckwith. He had already found her by the time I arrived up here. I called round on the pretext of renting a room; of course she told me she was full up but I persuaded her to allow me to leave my suitcase with her while I looked elsewhere for accommodation. I had a shrewd idea the Stantons were there because Mrs Beckwith was very agitated. As I walked down the street, I opened my handbag and took out a mirror. They were watching me from one of the rooms upstairs."

"And that's it?"

"Broadly speaking."

"Is your suitcase still there?"

She looked up at him, her face registering surprise. "Of course not," she said, "I collected it an hour or so later."

"And this was yesterday?"

"Of course."

"What am I supposed to do about the Stantons?"

"You are to kill them."

"Just like that?"

"Just like that."

"Without help from anyone?"

"Hunt has something organised."

"But you don't know the details?"

"I've no need to," she said casually.

Garnett leaned back against the wall and lit a cigarette while he mulled over dates and times. Coleman did not receive his letter until the first post yesterday morning. Barely twelve hours later Worsley had slipped the hotel reservation and a return ticket to York to him, yet Dane could not have left the office much before eleven which would put her time of arrival in York anywhere between three-thirty and five. Robinson had given him the word to go to Harry's Revue Bar at much the same time. It simply didn't add up.

"You seem worried about something?" said Dane.

"I am because it smells. All of it; you finding them so damn quick, the fact that they are still at large when they've been splashed

57

over every newspaper in the country and the best part of the national police force must be out looking for them. Then I am told to kill them, no question of trying to salvage anything from the mess; quite suddenly that doesn't matter anymore."

"I'm only a courier," she said calmly, "I just follow orders."

"I seem to remember Jodl used much the same line."

"Oh yes?" Dane said indifferently.

"It didn't do him much good, he was hanged at Nuremberg."

"Hadn't you better see Mr Hunt?" she said coldly.

"You really did miss your vocation," he said, "you should have been a schoolmistress." He walked out of the room slamming the door behind him.

Garnett found Hunt in the office nursing a glass of whisky. It wasn't exactly his first drink of the evening; he had that mellow look about him which arrives with the fifth or sixth glass. He was half sprawled in his chair, his gammy left leg propped up on a footstool. Twenty years ago he had had the reputation of being one of the hardest men in the game until someone put the boot in on his kneecap. He was perhaps luckier than most rugby league players; he'd had the good sense to marry a business woman. They had started by taking in lodgers and had now got as far as owning a small hotel. Hunt provided the local colour.

He looked up at Garnett and said, "I've been expecting you lad, pull up a chair." He waved his hand vaguely around the office. "There's a chair behind the door."

Garnett dragged the cane bottom chair out of its hiding place and sat down.

"About tomorrow?" said Garnett.

"Have a drink, it's good stuff, brewed it myself." He saw Garnett hesitate, and said, "Just a joke, Mr Daniel, it's the real thing straight from the black market."

"In that case, I'll join you."

"Straight, soda or water?"

"Soda, just a splash."

Hunt raised his glass, "Here's to a short war," he said.

"And a successful one."

"That goes without saying."

"About tomorrow?" Garnett repeated.

"Aye, well, we told London we'd give you as much help as we felt able to."

"And just how able are you feeling, Mr Hunt?"

"It could get a deal less every time you make what you think is a joke."

"All right, I'm sorry; let's try it from the beginning again."

Hunt picked up a box from the desk and flipped the lid open. "Have a cigar," he said, "all the way from Cuba, one of the benefits of a Co-prosperity Sphere."

Garnett took one, shaved off the end with his penknife and then lit it from the match Hunt was holding.

Between puffing on his cigar, Hunt said; "You've been told where to find them?"

"Forty-nine Tolcroft Road, right?"

Hunt contemplated the glowing tip of his cigar. "Correct," he said, "You also have been told it's a dead end street."

"So?"

"That's not quite correct. There's an alley between 59 and 60 which leads down to the river bank. You'll find a bridging site two hundred yards upstream from the alley. For some reason, the Russians left a class 30 bridge in after their engineer practice camp finished last fall. Lots of people make use of it. Once on the other side, you're in Thirsk Road. Half way up, in the direction of the A64, there's a greengrocer's, name of Chalmers. We'll have a light blue Zephyr waiting outside the shop from half past nine to ten. The driver will know where to take you."

"And if I don't make it on time?"

"That will be your bad luck."

"I've got a feeling I'm going to be dogged by it."

"What?"

"Bad luck. I've got to make six hundred metres before I reach the car and I've been given a gun which could waken the dead."

"Looking for an excuse to back out?"

Garnett leaned forward and tapped the cigar over an ashtray

labelled Souvenir of Scarborough. The hand painted picture of the castle and the harbour disappeared under a mountain of hot ash.

"I've never killed a woman before," he said slowly.

"It's a funny sort of war," said Hunt. He pointed at the print hanging on the wall. "See that? That's a Yorkshire Hussar, Officer, Full Dress 1897, cape, sabre, shako, silver braid, the lot. He thought he was going to ride into battle; seventeen years later he was minus his horse and waist deep in a waterlogged trench. There's a first time for everything."

"Only, you haven't got to do it."

"No, I haven't, but then we run things differently up here. We don't have to kill our own people. We run this town, we control the police, and the town council doesn't count for more than a row of beans. There isn't a thing going on that we don't know about in advance. That's how good our intelligence system is. We keep the Russians at arm's length and life goes on as normal."

"After tomorrow, it isn't going to be quite so normal."

"There are still sex crimes."

"What is that supposed to mean?"

"After you have done your bit, we're going to make it look as if it was a normal run of the mill murder—nothing to do with the Resistance whatsoever."

"It won't work," said Garnett, "the police are after them for the assassination of Blythe."

"Don't you worry about that. That's our problem."

"How do I get to Tolcroft Road?"

"You make your own way."

Garnett swallowed the rest of the whisky and mashed the cigar butt in the ashtray. "I suppose I can count on the Zephyr being there?" he said.

Hunt stared at him open mouthed. Eventually he said, "That's a damn fool question, isn't it? We're playing this just the way London wants it."

"I expect you're right."

"You've got nothing to worry about."

"That's a comfort," said Garnett. He said goodnight and went up to his room.

Dane wasn't there of course but she had left the street map on the bed for him to study. In a fit of bad temper, he picked up the map and flung it across the room. Still in a temper, he brushed his teeth, undressed quickly and slipped in between the cold sheets.

He put the light out but sleep didn't come easily. Certain phrases bothered Garnett and he couldn't put them out of his mind. "You are to kill them—Just like that?—I'm only a courier—The car will be there from half past nine to ten—if you miss it that's your bad luck—There are still sex crimes—it's going to look as if it was a normal run of the mill murder—we're playing this just the way London wants it—you're becoming hot—Does that mean you plan to rest me?—I don't know, perhaps."

Tomorrow is going to be a balls up, he thought drowsily, just like that first job. Where was it? Salisbury, yes that was it, Salisbury, early summer, first year of Soviet occupation, four months after he had broken out of Parkhurst. The target was Willie Vosper, Commissar of Wiltshire. Garnett drifted off to sleep.

They waited for Vosper in the market square, standing innocently in the bus queue near the street corner, where they knew his car would have to slow down to negotiate the sharp bend. Garnett carried a raincoat over his arm to conceal the Sterling sub machine gun.

It was a fine clear morning. A policeman loitered on the opposite side of the street. A milk float whirred by, and three schoolgirls in blazers and white boaters at the head of the queue giggled over some private joke. A man behind him remarked, to no one in particular, that it was a nice day.

Vosper's Humber crawled into view. Garnett dropped the mac and pointed the SMG at the windscreen. The gun coughed twice and then jammed. He re-cocked, shook out the damaged round and squeezed the trigger again. The bolt slid forward jamming once more.

His companion was shouting obscenities as he blazed away with a Smith and Wesson .38 revolver. The policeman started to run across the road towards them, the schoolgirls screamed and the man behind

Garnett made a half hearted attempt to grapple with him. The Humber stalled opposite their position in the bus queue.

There was a separated cartridge case in the barrel which Garnett couldn't budge. In desperation he flung the Sterling at the Humber, smashing the zone toughened windscreen. Snatching the Browning Automatic out of the shoulder holster, Garnett whipped round and slashed the barrel across the face of the man behind him, who, though he was pretty ineffectual, was still giving him a certain amount of trouble.

Garnett turned again, wrenched open the front door of the car and leaned inside. The chauffeur, bleeding from a bullet wound in the shoulder, was trying to start the engine, the bodyguard still had one leg in the car. Vosper, a small insignificant little man, stared at Garnett through thick pebble glasses. The chauffeur decided discretion was the better part of valour; he got out of the car in a hurry.

Garnett shot Vosper in the face and then again in the chest as he fell back in his seat. He ducked out of the car and ran diagonally across the road towards the car park where the car was waiting. Seeing the gun in his hand, the uniformed policeman veered away from him, but, glancing back over his shoulder, Garnett saw that Vosper's bodyguard had cut off his companion. He stopped running, turned about and fired three shots in quick succession at the uniformed policeman who looked as though he had now plucked up enough balls to have a go at him.

In the confusion, his companion almost made it. He was running towards Garnett when the bodyguard hit him in the neck. For a few paces his stride remained unchecked even though the blood was spurting from the hole in his throat, and then, quite suddenly, he collapsed like a rag doll.

The Wolsley roared out of the car park and came to a halt a few yards beyond Garnett. Someone shouted to him and he backed away towards the car, still firing at the bodyguard crouching beside the Humber. A bullet glanced off the road and struck one of the schoolgirls. Her screams were the last thing Garnett heard as he leapt into the Wolsley.

Garnett woke up with a start, his mouth dry and heart thumping, not certain where he was for the moment. He fumbled with the light switch and sat up in bed. "It was just a bad dream," he muttered.

Think of something else, he told himself. Like what? Like Elizabeth. Remember a warm summer's evening, the two of you just back from a drinks' party. Liz in the kitchen standing in front of the gas stove, asking if you feel like eating. You don't feel like it, just a cup of coffee. She has her back to you, and there is this zip which stretches from her neck all the way down to her hips. You kiss the nape of her neck, and the zip moves easily and your other hand slips inside the dress and cups a well rounded firm breast which fills the palm. And Elizabeth says, hey, stop that, what do you think you're doing, but she doesn't mean it, and she turns to face you, and you have to withdraw your hand. Her arms go round your neck, and her mouth is warm, open, and inviting, and you feel her hard up against you, and she is breathing quickly. You break apart and gently slip the dress off her shoulders, and then the straps of her slip, and her eyes widen, and she whispers—not in here, and she takes you by the hand and you follow her into the lounge, and she is walking with quick, urgent, short steps. And God there is nothing so wonderful as Liz in heat, and her arms seem to crush you and her teeth are sharp, and afterwards you are lying there spent and exhausted, and Liz, amused, says—aren't we depraved—and you can hear the man next door mowing his lawn and you say—isn't it a good job I forgot to cut the hedge and she laughs. And the milk is boiling over on the stove and neither of you cares.

But Liz is dead.

7

Garnett decided to walk, not because the morning was mild and inviting, but because he wanted to get the feel of the city. There might come a time when he would need to know every twist and turn, every lane and alley, and to rely on a detailed study of a street plan just wasn't good enough.

He walked leisurely because he was in no hurry. The morning rush hour traffic flowed round and past him, quick moving pedestrians, and a horde of cyclists sometimes three abreast, weaving in and out of the buses and trucks. There were a few private cars about but not many: petrol rationing saw to that.

Garnett first became aware of the traffic hold up as he came into Parliament Street. As far as the eye could see nothing was moving, and the crowds were piling up on the pavements. He made his way down Piccadilly until he reached the head of the crowd on the corner of Fulford and Piccadilly and then the reason for the hold up became clear.

A coil of wire had been looped across the road to form a crude but effective barrier. Behind it stood four Russian soldiers casually menacing the crowd with their 7.62mm Kalashnikov AKM assault rifles. Two uniformed policemen stood some distance apart from the Russians trying to give the impression that they were not collaborators. Their pretence was wasted.

Snatches of subdued conversation reached Garnett but he could make little sense of it. Without turning his head, Garnett spoke to the man at his elbow. "Any idea what is going on?" he asked.

"They say a couple of Russians have been shot in the Fulford Road, and they're rounding up hostages." The man spoke out of the corner of his mouth in a low pitched monotone, slurring each word and running it into the next, making what he said unintelligible.

Garnett could hear the faint throb of diesel engines in the distance. A voice from the back said, "Sounds as if they are coming this way," and the crowd shuffled uneasily. Seconds later, a BTR 60p eight wheeled amphibious armoured personnel carrier passed them, moving in the direction of the castle. Garnett counted twelve such vehicles, six in front and six in rear of the eight ZIL 157 cargo trucks. The trucks were loaded with civilians.

The same voice said; "About two hundred then, they must be taking them out to the barracks at Strensall."

As the last of the convoy disappeared from view, the soldiers dragged the barbed wire to one side and waved the traffic on.

Fulford Road was as dead as the two Russian soldiers. The shops were closed up tight and no one else was about with the exception of Garnett and the militia sentry who stood duty outside the Second British Corps Headquarters. He noticed that the flag above the entrance was flying at half mast. That this apology for an army should mourn the death of an enemy was no more than he expected.

The brooding silence was broken by five MIG 26 VTOL fighter bombers which swept in low over the city scattering a cloud of leaflets from their fat bellies. At the end of their run, they broke formation and fanned out like the fingers on a spread hand, climbed sharply, rolled over, changed geometric configuration and on the reverse course, broke through the sound barrier. The sonic boom rocked buildings and cracked windows. The militia sentry caught Garnett's eye and smiled nervously. He at least was impressed by this show of force. The leaflets fluttered slowly to earth and came to rest in alleys, lanes, streets, parks, gardens, trees and on the rooftops themselves. Garnett did not have to see one to know what it contained; he was familiar with the mixture of threats, cajolery, and blatant lies which were the hallmarks of Soviet propóganda.

Forty-nine Tolcroft Road was no different from the other fifty-nine yellow bricked, slate roofed Victorian houses which made up the street, except that the front garden was overgrown and the rotting window frames hadn't seen a lick of paint in years. Garnett opened the side gate and went round to the kitchen. The milk was still on the back door step. He rang the bell and waited.

The door opened a fraction of an inch and a woman spoke through the crack. "What do you want?" she said nervously.

"Police," he said abruptly, "come on, open up." It didn't sound very convincing to his ears but the woman complied meekly enough.

"Police you say?" she said suspiciously. Watery eyes blinked at him from behind steel framed spectacles.

"Mrs Beckwith?" he queried.

She nodded. A pink tongue flicked out and moistened the lower lip. She passed a hand quickly across her forehead, brushing a strand of grey hair back off her face. "What do you want now?" she said. Her voice and manner were surly because she didn't want Garnett to see that she was afraid.

"A young couple you've been hiding. Their name's Stanton." Her mouth opened to deny it but Garnett cut her short. "Don't bother to lie," he said wearily, "We know they're here."

"You'd better come in then."

He accepted her grudging invitation. And now that he was inside the house, standing in the gloomy kitchen, looking across a square table covered by a dirty, grease-stained tablecloth at this frump of a woman with her fat legs, swollen ankles, double chins, and calculating watery blue eyes; now he had come this far he knew he could no longer shut the problem out of his mind. In a few minutes, this avaricious woman would lead him to them; a man and a woman whom he had never seen, never even spoken to, had no personal quarrel with, and these were the people he was supposed to kill with about as much emotion as he would experience in swatting the life out of a fly. And he knew that if they stood there and did absolutely nothing to defend themselves, he could no more squeeze the trigger in cold blood than he could bring himself to smother a helpless child in a cot.

Beckwith folded her arms over her ample bosom. "You're not one of the local coppers, are you?" she said.

"Suppose you show me to their room?"

"First the Russians and then you," she grumbled, "I don't know what things are coming to these days." She stumped out of the

66

room, her large bottom waggling from side to side.

The hall was papered over with something which looked like purple roses on a cream background, brass rungs held a threadbare staircarpet in place, and on the landing upstairs, he noticed a glass framed tapestry of the child in the manger, which said, God bless this house, Harriet Sawyer, aged eleven years, August 1872.

Beckwith stopped outside a dark stained door and said, "This is their room."

She looked at him expectantly and Garnett signalled her to open the door. He slipped the automatic out of the shoulder holster, flicked the safety off and thumbed the hammer back before he followed her into the bedroom.

The girl was lying on the bed watching the smoke from her cigarette curl up towards the ceiling. As a smoke ring appeared, she jabbed her finger through it and appeared to get a kick out of doing it.

Garnett said affably, "Hullo Jean, where's Derek?"

She was a lot thinner than he had expected. Her collar bones stuck out painfully and her face had a pinched look. Her chest was very nearly as flat as a board. She turned on to her side to face him, and she was very calm, so calm in fact that Garnett thought she was fey.

"Didn't Aunty Kath tell you?" she said. "They took him for a hostage." She giggled nervously, "He was hiding in the closet under the stairs. He looked so funny standing there with the mops and brooms all around him."

A sinking feeling started in the pit of his stomach. A premonition that it was going to be a foul up was now confirmed.

Beckwith said, "This man is from the police."

Stanton swung her feet on to the floor and burst out laughing. "My God," she spluttered, "you are naïve. He's one of them."

"One of who?"

"The Resistance. He's probably come to settle the score."

The colour mounted in Beckwith's face and she rounded on Garnett. "Now, look here," she said, waving a finger in front of his face, "you've no right to force your way into my house making out that you're a bloody policeman. I've got a good mind to send for a real policeman, and then where would you be?"

"In trouble like you."

"Like me?" Her voice rose an octave, "why should I be in trouble, I've done nothing wrong."

"A man called Blythe was killed three days ago. Her husband was involved, I'd call that trouble enough."

"I didn't know about that."

"You'd have to be deaf, dumb and blind to get away with that excuse."

Beckwith collapsed on to the bed and looked up at him with her mouth half open.

"What are we going to do?" she whispered.

Garnett tucked the Remington back into the shoulder holster. "I think it would be a good thing if they didn't find her here, because, make no mistake, her husband has about as much chance of remaining undetected as I have of becoming Prime Minister. I wouldn't be in your shoes if the Russians do come back, you'd have a lot of explaining to do. With her out of the way, you can lie in your teeth, and it's only Stanton's word against yours."

The argument was full of holes but she was prepared to grasp at any straw. Her eyes took on a thoughtful look and he knew that he had won her over to his side.

"I think you had better do as he says, Jean."

Stanton shrugged her shoulders expressively. "Well that's it then, isn't it?" she said. "I mean as long as you are all right. Aunty Kath, it doesn't matter what happens to me."

"We're not related," Beckwith said coldly.

"You bloody old cow, since when have I ceased to be your niece?"

"I was just a friend of your mother's."

"Some friend," said Stanton. She got up from the bed and took her coat out of the wardrobe and held it out to Garnett.

"You don't need any help," he said.

"You have such nice manners," she said bitingly.

"I'm just cautious. I knew a man who was sent to bring in a

68

suspected double agent. He was a gentleman, well mannered especially where the opposite sex were concerned. The girl persuaded him to hold the coat for her so that she could slip into it, and when he was standing there like a valet, she shot him in the stomach."

"You know the nicest people," she said.

Stanton buttoned up the coat, picked up her handbag and walked out of the room without so much as a backward glance.

Tolcroft Road still had a Sunday look about it; just about everyone had, it seemed, decided to stay indoors. The faint breeze which had sprung up caught Stanton's fine black hair and swept it about her face; occasionally she would brush it out of her eyes but it didn't appear to bother her overmuch. Judging by the set of her chin and composure, Garnett thought nothing bothered her any more.

In a matter of fact voice, she said; "This path leads to the river."

Garnett made no comment.

"Are you planning to push me into the river?" Her voice was flat and unnaturally calm. "It won't do you any good, you know, I'm a strong swimmer."

"That's comforting, I can hardly swim a stroke."

"Why don't you get it over with?"

"You've got an unhealthy fixation about death."

"Aren't you going to kill me then?"

"What would be the point of that?"

She shrugged her shoulders. "Not much, but then I'm not a mind reader."

They crossed the river by the pontoon bridge and walked up Thirsk Road. Chalmer's, the greengrocers, were doing a brisk trade. A queue stretched out of the shop on to the pavement. There was no sign of a light blue Zephyr, but that hardly surprised Garnett.

"What's your name?" she said suddenly.

"What?"

"Your name, didn't you hear?"

"Daniel, David Daniel."

"It's more original than Smith." She tossed her head, "It's not your real name, of course. I suppose there must be times when even

69

you have difficulty in knowing who you really are."

There's a lot of truth in that, thought Garnett.

"You look lost," she said, "don't you know what to do?"

He stopped outside the call box at the top of the road. "I think I'll make a call," he said.

"You don't seem very sure of yourself."

Garnett opened the door of the phone booth and pushed her inside. He chose to ignore her last remark because the truth was that he was not at all sure what to do. He inserted a fivepenny piece into the coin box and half turned his back on her so that she couldn't see him dial the number. He got Hunt on the line.

Garnett said; "I wonder if you would take a message for my associate. Would you please say that I am unable to close the deal because the senior partner is not available. I am however in close touch with the other interested party, and will call back in half an hour for further instructions."

He hung up before Hunt had a chance to reply.

"They're not going to like that," she said smugly.

"I don't suppose they will." He took hold of her arm and led her outside.

They walked slowly back towards the city by way of Micklebar Gate and the Ouse Bridge. If the pictures in the guide books were anything to go by, York had once been a show place but now it was beginning to look seedy and run down. Litter hung about in the gutters and most of the shops, which were still in business, looked as if they could do with a coat of paint.

A prowl car cruised by slowly, the loud hailer on the roof metallically spewing out an ultimatum. Garnett noticed that not a single person looked at the car, everyone it seemed was determined to ignore its existence. The police car pulled up outside a fish and chip shop and repeated the message.

"Two hundred hostages because two Russians are dead," she whispered. "My God, how can you hope to win?"

Garnett thought she had a point. Measured in those terms, theirs was a lost cause.

"Will they execute all of them?"

70

"Maybe," he said absently.

He noticed that she was clenching and unclenching her hands. Now and then she would glance back over her shoulder as if she expected to find someone on their heels.

In an effort to reassure her, Garnett said; "It's all right, we're not being followed, nothing is going to happen to you."

"I wish I could believe that," she said in a small voice.

He stopped outside a coffee bar. "You need a drink," he said.

"I don't."

"Well I do," he insisted. Garnett opened the door and pushed her inside.

The bar was a psychedelic experience; shades of orange, green and purple dazzled the eyes wherever you looked. A couple of teenagers deep in conversation, and a man in a dirty mac whose face was hidden behind the *Morning Star* were the only occupants. The decor probably accounted for the lack of trade.

Garnett selected a table at the back, fed some loose change into the juke box and then went over to the self service counter. A lank haired man served him coffee in white Pyrex cups. The coffee was as pale as the cup it came in.

She toyed with the coffee which was understandable because it tasted lousy. Garnett lit two cigarettes and gave one to Stanton.

"Thanks," she said nervously, "I was dying for one." She drew on the cigarette hungrily and said, "What will happen to Derek?"

"I wish I knew."

"You're afraid he will talk." She leaned forward, her face white and tense, "He won't, you know. He can't tell them anything without disclosing who he is. Either way he is in bad trouble."

"I think you need a stiff drink."

"Why don't you let me go? I won't betray you."

Garnett stood up and walked back to the counter. He smiled wanly at the lank haired waiter. "My wife's had some bad news," he said softly, "her mother you see."

"Dead?"

"Dying. Cancer."

The waiter glanced across the room at Stanton. "That's awful," he said sympathetically.

"I wondered if you would have anything which might steady her nerves a bit?"

The waiter disappeared below the counter and groped inside the cupboard. Presently he stood up and placed a cup in front of Garnett.

Garnett eyed the odourless drink suspiciously. "What's in it?" he asked quietly.

"Industrial alcohol and orange juice, it's quite safe."

"I'll take your word for it. What do I owe you?"

"Nothing, it's on the house." He leaned forward and whispered, "Haven't you been here before?"

"It could be, we live in Fulford."

The man snapped his fingers. "Of course, that's it," he said, "I knew I'd seen your wife somewhere, I live in Malton Crescent."

Garnett moved away. "Do you now," he said, "that's a coincidence, we live round the corner from Malton Crescent." She was drowning the cigarette butt in the coffee when he came back. He thrust the drink at her and said; "Here, drink this, it will do you the power of good."

The raw spirit brought tears to her eyes. "God," she breathed, "what was that?"

"Industrial alcohol, it's guaranteed not to send you blind. Are you feeling better?"

"Why? Are we going someplace?"

"It's time I checked in again."

"You're worried," she said, "go on admit it. You're frightened."

"All right, I'm frightened. Does that also help to make you feel better?"

"Oh yes, it does. I'm glad you are afraid because now you know what it is like."

"So, I'm scared," he said, "if they pick us up, we'll both die laughing. Now let's get the hell out of here."

He walked her up to the market place in search of a phone booth. Garnett had a nasty feeling that Hunt was going to let him stew in his own juice and the idea made him jumpy. It also annoyed him

72

that Stanton was getting a kick out of his obvious discomfort. He thrust her into the first vacant call box they came to and rang the hotel. They were a long time answering.

"No one at home?" she suggested cheerfully.

The ringing tone stopped and in the silence which followed he could hear someone breathing into the phone. Garnett said; "Hullo? Is anyone there?"

"This is the Northern General Hospital, can I help you?" The voice was Dane's.

"My name is Daniel."

"Oh yes, Mr Daniel, we've been expecting you to call back. We have managed to find your wife a private room in Women's Surgical. Would you please ensure she reports to reception between eleven-thirty and twelve this morning."

"Thank you," said Garnett, "you've been most helpful." He rang off and checked the address of the hospital in the directory.

"What did they say?" she asked.

"You're to go into hospital."

The faint smile on her lips drained away. "Why?"

"Can you think of a better place to hide?"

"Hospitals make me nervous; they have operating theatres and a mortuary."

"Nothing is going to happen to you."

"So you keep on saying." She paused and then said, "I'll need nightclothes, toilet articles, suitcase, things like that. Shall we go back for them?"

"I'll buy you everything you need. I've got the necessary clothing coupons."

"How wonderful to be in your shoes." she said dryly.

8

She was sitting up in bed, the pink bed jacket draped loosely about her shoulders, her eyes half closed and a faint smile on her lips as though she was enjoying a private joke.

Garnett said; "I've only got a few minutes."

"I'm not keeping you," she said.

Garnett lit two cigarettes and gave one to her. "There are a couple of things I have to know," he said.

"What makes you think I'd tell you anything?"

"Because I don't think you're tired of living. I know you locked Pollard in the Swainsons' flat and I want to know why?"

She shrugged her shoulders. "He told Derek no harm would come to Swainson. It was a lie, of course, and when Derek discovered this, he went a little crazy. Locking Pollard in was done on the spur of the moment. It was his way of getting even."

"And then what?"

"We came straight up here, because we didn't know where else to hide."

"You got here the same day?"

She blew a smoke ring towards the ceiling. "About six in the evening."

"And your aunt took you in?"

"For a consideration; four hundred pounds' worth of consideration to be precise." She smiled lopsidedly. "She was telling the truth when she said she wasn't my aunt. She was just a friend of my mother's."

"Where did you get that kind of money?" Garnett said sharply.

"Pollard. He provided a car and five hundred pounds. We abandoned the car in Regent's Park."

74

"And the bookshop?"

"What about it?"

"It was a message centre. I want a list of your contacts."

"Three months ago I could have told you, but then Pollard dispersed the groups and switched the channels of communication. He wanted us for the bank job."

It was just possible she was telling the truth. It had been public knowledge for several weeks that someone high up in the government would come down to officially open the new Cadet Police College. Pollard would have spent months planning that job, and not unnaturally he would want his team isolated and protected from everyday risks. However the slack expression on her face wasn't giving anything away and she could have been lying in her teeth for all he knew.

The door opened without warning and an auburn haired girl of twenty-six or thereabouts flounced into the room. For a uniform she wore a long white coat; she could have been a social worker, or a physiotherapist, or a dietician or even a doctor. She smiled quickly at Garnett, and, without saying a word, opened the wardrobe and took out the cheap fibre suitcase which he had bought in the market. She gathered up Stanton's clothes and bundled them into the suitcase.

The way she glanced at her wristwatch was obvious, and it didn't surprise him when she said; "I'm afraid I will have to ask you to leave now, Mr Daniel. Visiting hours are from six to seven except on Sunday when it's two to four-thirty."

Garnett stubbed his cigarette out in the ashtray, got up out of the chair and picked up the suitcase. He nodded at Stanton and said, "I'll see you tonight."

Stanton made no reply. She knew as well as Garnett did that, without her clothes, she wasn't going anywhere.

Markham was waiting for him on the steps outside the front entrance to the hospital. He came up behind Garnett and grabbed hold of his right elbow, digging his nails into the tendons so that Garnett was unable to move his arm.

"We want a word with you," he whispered.

75

"So it seems. Are we going somewhere?"

"We're going to have a talk with Hunt. We are not pinching you if that's what you're worried about."

"Then why hang on to my arm?"

Markham said; "I know you've got a gun. I didn't want you to jump to any hasty conclusions; I've heard you act first and think later. The car is over this way."

The arm felt much better when Markham let go of it but he still had no strength in the hand, and Garnett made a mental note not to quarrel with him if he could help it. The car was a pale blue Vauxhall Viva. Halliday was sitting glumly behind the wheel.

"Do you two always work together?" said Garnett.

Markham took the suitcase out of his hand and dumped it in the trunk. "We're a good team," he said, "you might say we are complementary. Jack's good with his eyes, he can spot a wrong un a mile off, and I've got the silver tongue."

He ushered Garnett into the back of the car and sat beside him. Halliday fired the Vauxhall into life and drove out of the car park.

Markham held out his hand and smiled encouragingly. "You won't be needing the gun now," he said cheerfully.

"I'm not in danger, is that it?"

"You never have been."

"That's a matter of opinion. I think I will hang on to it for a while longer. You don't mind do you?"

"Not at all, have it your way," said Markham.

The smile was still there but it was a little strained.

Nobody said a word. They came into the city through Monkbar, skirted the Minster, crossed the Lendal Bridge and went up past the station. At Micklebar they turned into the Leeds Road and then filtered on to the A59 beyond a derelict cinema. Shop signs flashed by; absently he noticed a corn and seed merchant called Hardacre, a hoarding advertising Birds Eye Peas and an undertaker with the friendly name of Death.

Light rain began to fall from a darkening sky. The windscreen wipers smeared the traffic film, making it difficult for Halliday to see properly. He tried pumping the washers but the reservoir was

76

empty. The road passed above the railway marshalling yards and then led them past street after street of semi detacheds. The street they eventually turned into was no different from any other except that it was known as Grenville Drive.

The small red brick house had bay windows and mock Tudor beams fanning out like the rays of the sun in the gables. The owner evidently took pride in the appearance of the front garden. The lawn was well kept and free of weeds; a neat evergreen hedge gave the house some privacy. Hunt was waiting for them on the doorstep; a Hillman Husky was parked on the garage front.

He ushered Garnett and Markham into the parlour which was a small enough room in its own right without the clutter of furniture which made it seem even smaller. Potted plants standing in chipped saucers covered the top of the upright piano, a sofa took up most of one wall, whilst facing it were two armchairs, and a card table, which stood in the centre of the room because there was no place else for it to go. A Westminster clock perched precariously on the narrow mantelpiece above the gas fire. Dane occupied one of the armchairs. Nobody bothered to remove their coats.

Hunt said, "I hear you delivered the girl to the hospital without any trouble; at least that's your little problem solved."

"I wouldn't go so far as to say that," said Garnett, "at least not while her husband remains in their hands."

"He's just one of two hundred and to be frank, the other one hundred and ninety-nine concern me a hell of a lot more than does your precious Mr Stanton." Hunt paused, turned to Markham and said, "What have we got on the killing?"

Markham stopped picking at his teeth with a matchstick. "Not much," he said laconically, "all we know is that these two Russians were walking along the Fulford Road towards the British militia barracks when a youth on a bicycle rode up behind them and shot them through the head with a .22 target pistol."

"Any chance of finding him?"

Markham snapped the matchstick in half between his fingers. "Not unless someone tips us off," he said.

Garnett said, "Do I hear right? You are thinking of helping the

Russians to find this youth?"

Hunt's face began to turn a delicate shade of pink. "This killing wasn't planned by us, and two hundred people are going to die unless we do something about it." His voice faded to a mumble; "We just can't stand by and do nothing."

Markham was looking at a print of the Shambles on the wall above the mantelpiece which seemed to interest him. "If it's a killer we're after," he said thoughtfully, "why don't we stick to the original plan?"

Hunt looked down at the carpet and then slowly raised his head. He met Garnett's cold stare and glanced away. "The situation has changed," he said harshly.

Garnett said; "What situation?"

"It's obvious, isn't it?" said Hunt. "We're talking about Stanton. If he had been available we might have had an angle."

"You could make a trade, one of their kind for our two hundred."

Hunt began to look interested. "What have you got in mind?" he said.

"We could grab the District Commander or someone close to him like his wife, or son or daughter, it doesn't matter too much who it is, as long as the person is sufficiently important to give us a lever."

Markham laughed harshly. "Listen," he said, "you don't know what you're talking about. The District Commander lives out at Claxton Hall with a platoon of soldiers to guard him, and his family happens to be in Moscow. And finally, we don't happen to have a team which is strong enough to take on that kind of opposition."

Garnett said, "I wasn't thinking in terms of a local Resistance Group."

"The nearest commando was based on Warcop which is over eighty miles from here." Hunt paused and then said, "The Russians had themselves a partridge drive last November which took care of most of them. I would have thought even London had heard about that."

The silence which followed was broken by the Westminster clock chiming the quarter hour.

Garnett cleared his throat and said; "It seems to me we have two options open. We can either hope the youth will give himself up, or the Russians will be magnanimous. Killing two hundred men as a reprisal isn't going to improve their popularity. Whatever happens, I personally think they will settle for twenty if only to make the point that there is no percentage in killing a Russian."

"Perhaps we could buy them off."

"You could try. It occurs to me that there is still one other possible solution. It may be that Stanton is still at large. After all we've only got Beckwith's word he was taken hostage."

Markham said, "Let's turn her place over then."

"Officially," Garnett said coldly, "the police aren't supposed to know she was hiding them, and we have to be sure he is still in circulation before we make a move. I suggest you check out the list of hostages. If Stanton has been taken, he probably gave a false name and address."

"And if he is not on the list, what then?"

"I have another talk with Beckwith and then we go looking for him."

"All right," said Hunt, "but understand this, when and if we find Stanton, we hand him over D.O.A. to the Russians."

"You won't hear any objections from me," said Garnett.

Markham shook his head in disbelief. "If you're thinking that you can fool the Russians into believing we've caught their killer for them, may I remind you there is a little matter of ballistics."

Garnett said, "They were shot with a .22. Providing the lead bullet struck bone, ballistics will have nothing to go on. It might be an idea to get hold of the rounds from post mortem before ballistics do if there's still time. You can always flatten them out a little bit before you hand them over."

Hunt said, "While you're at it, get a hold of a .22 target pistol just in case we do find Stanton. It'll look more convincing if the right gun is found on his body." He turned to Garnett and said, "You stay here with the girl for the time being. We'll be in touch."

"I don't want anything to happen to Jean Stanton before we get our hands on him. Do I make myself clear?"

Hunt smiled for the first time that morning. Lapsing into dialect, he said, "I'll say one thing for thee lad, thou's not lacking in cheek."

He limped out of the room on Markham's heels and closed the door behind him. The front door slammed; a minute or so later, first one car and then the other throbbed into life.

Dane slid out of her chair and knelt in front of the gas fire. "It's cold in here," she said, hugging her arms around her body. "Have you got a match?"

Garnett dropped a box of Swan Vestas into her lap. She was wearing a dark blue suit and the short skirt had ridden up her thighs exposing a lot of eye catching leg. He promised himself that one of these days he was going to find out if this occasional peep show was deliberate or accidental.

The gas fire hissed and popped under the match, and eventually settled down to a steady roar as she got the hang of adjusting the tap. Garnett slipped his mac off and draped it over the back of an armchair.

She looked up to return the Swan Vestas and saw the expression on his face. "Is something wrong?" she asked.

Put like that, it sounded banal. She might have been the little woman welcoming the bread winner home and asking him what sort of a day he had had at the office.

"You were a great help," he said.

"I don't understand."

"Just now, when Markham nearly let the cat out of the bag."

"I still don't understand."

"The young one with the yellow hair; he's Markham. Surely you've met him before?"

"Not until today."

"He has a friend, tall, very thin, with a sad looking face. Perhaps he was the one you saw yesterday?"

"I met Mr Hunt yesterday," she said in a level voice, "and no one else."

"Did you show him a photograph of me?"

Her eyes opened wide. "Of course not. Why should I? I hadn't the faintest idea that you were in the Resistance until I walked into your room last night. I wish you would tell me what you are driving at."

"I wish I knew," said Garnett. "You said Hunt had already located the Stantons by the time you arrived?"

"Yes, that's right. Mr Coleman sent their description ahead by telex."

"And you believe that?"

"Well, is there any reason not to?"

"Hell, I don't know," he said angrily. "I have a feeling that the only thing which went over on the telex was a run down on D. Garnett Esq. including the time I was expected to arrive in York."

She got up from the floor and placed the matches on the mantelpiece. "I think I had better find something for us to eat," she said.

She started to move away, but Garnett caught hold of her and pulled her back. She was standing very close to him and it seemed natural to slip his arms around her waist and draw her closer. Her lips turned up in a smile which was reflected in her eyes. Her mouth opened under his; their bodies collided.

"This beats fighting any day," he murmured.

9

The faint light thrown off by the gas fire showed a jumble of discarded clothing lying on the carpet. She nestled beside him on the couch, one leg resting on his hip, the sensuous smile betraying the demure look in her eyes. His hand encircling her breast felt the nipple grow hard under his touch.

"Don't you ever get tired of it?" she whispered.

"Do you?"

"Not when it is as good as this."

She moved her leg, running her foot down the outside of his calf, a sharp fingernail traced the pattern of the white scar on his chest, causing the flesh to ripple involuntarily.

"How did you get this?" she asked quietly.

"Trying to get through the cordon around Bristol." He paused and then said; for no good reason, "I was trying to find out what had happened to my wife and son."

The fingernail stopped moving and she seemed to draw away from him. "I didn't know you were married," she said softly.

"There was no occasion to mention it before now."

"Tell me about them."

"Why?"

"Because I am curious. I can't compete with ghosts."

Garnett stretched out a hand and grabbing his pants, found a crumpled packet of cigarettes and the box of matches in one of the pockets. He lit a cigarette, and leaned back staring up at the ceiling, his head resting on one arm.

Presently, he said, "Her name was Elizabeth and she's been dead for over four years. If you asked me to describe her now, I recall she was dark, slim, and I suppose you could say extremely attractive.

She was nineteen when we got married, and we had a son within a year. The boy was seven when he died. If you're good at mental arithmetic, you'll know we had eight years together. Perhaps the word together is a bit misleading. There were periods of separation because of the nature of my job. Some of them couldn't be avoided, but there were occasions when she could have followed me, but we had this house in Keynsham which was near her mother."

"I see," Dane said quietly.

"I don't think you do. She wasn't tied to her mother's apron strings. Far from it, she just wasn't cut out to be the wife of a serving officer. Elizabeth hated the life, she thought it narrow. I've often wondered what would have happened to us both if that situation had persisted."

He drew on the cigarette and then pinched it out between his fingers. "When I found out they were dead, I began to wish I had been shot with all the other officers who had surrendered."

Dane stirred and their hips touched. "How did you manage to avoid it?" she said.

"I'd heard about Katyn."

"Katyn?" she said vaguely.

"A place in Russia where the Wehrmacht uncovered the graves of ten thousand Polish officers murdered on Stalin's orders. I tore my badges of rank off before I went into the bag. Do you know why I went on escaping?"

"No."

"Because I didn't have the nerve to kill myself and I wanted them to do it for me."

"And now?"

"And now I'm glad to be alive and I don't want to die."

He rolled over towards her and sought out her mouth. His hand touched her flank and caressed it.

"Hey," she protested, "you're insatiable."

The front door bell rang. Dane sat bolt upright and stared at Garnett.

"Markham," he said, "two to one it's Markham." He rolled off the couch and started pulling on his clothes.

83

"For God's sake," said Dane, "give me a chance to get into the kitchen before you open the door to him." She scooped up her clothes, slipped her bare feet into her shoes and stumbled out of the room.

Garnett finished dressing, put the light on and took a quick look around the room. He noticed a square of white nylon on the carpet, picked it up and shoved it into his jacket pocket before he went to the front door. Markham was standing on the doorstep, his coat collar turned up against the steady drizzle.

Garnett said, "Are you alone or is someone with you?"

"The car is parked round the corner, Halliday is looking after it."

"Why don't you come in out of the rain?"

"All right, just for a minute though while you get yourself ready."

"You've checked out the list of hostages?"

"Correct," said Markham. "Two hundred names on the list and we've accounted for all of them. Stanton wasn't among them, but they did take one man from 49 Tolcroft Road."

Garnett said, "I'll get my mac. Have you checked the hospital?"

"What for?"

"We ought to make sure we still have his wife."

"You have a point there," Markham conceded.

Garnett went into the front room, picked up his mac and then went into the kitchen. Dane had finished dressing and was standing in front of the stove waiting for the kettle to come to the boil. He pulled the pair of panties out of his jacket pocket and pushed them into Dane's hand. "Present for you," he said, "before you catch a cold." She took them without batting an eyelid.

"Are you off somewhere?" she said.

"I've just been told Stanton isn't among the hostages. Markham and I are going to check the hospital."

She turned the gas out. "Do you want me to come along?"

"I think you ought to call London to let them know what's happened. I'll keep in touch with you as and when I can."

"Take care of yourself then," she said.

Her concern surprised him and for a moment he was lost for a

84

reply. "And you," he said lamely.

He joined Markham, walked to the car and got in the back. The rain didn't seem to be easing off and under the orange street lamps the road became a black satin ribbon stretching before them as far as the eye could see. It was a quiet night, the streets were empty, and the traffic on the police radio net was minimal. It was the sort of night when you didn't mind having to stay indoors.

Markham said; "Looks as though the curfew is one hundred per cent this time."

"Aye, they mean business," said Halliday. And as if to confirm his opinion they ran into two separate army patrols in as many minutes and heard the sound of gunfire in the distance.

Halliday pulled into the visitors' car park at the Northern General and cut the engine. Half turning to face Markham, he said, "Who's going to mind the car?"

"You are," said Markham. "We shan't be long."

Heels clacking a staccato beat on the uneven asphalt, they walked across the empty yard towards Reception. Their approaching footsteps dragged the hall porter away from his newspaper and forced him to get up out of his chair. He was an old man and he did not take kindly to their intrusion. "Visiting hour was from six to seven," he said testily.

Markham produced his ID card and waved it at the old man as they went past him. "That's different then," he shouted after them, "you can come in." He went back to the sports page vastly relieved.

Blue indicator arrows led them through distempered corridors to the Women's Surgical Ward where a nightlight was burning in the Sister's office. Markham tapped on the rippled glass window, and opened the door.

"Not at home," he said, withdrawing his head, "she must be going round the ward."

"Can I help you?"

The speaker had a Southern Irish accent, and turning, Garnett came face to face with a small dark woman in her late thirties. The name tag on her apron read Pearce.

Markham said; "We're police officers, Sister. We'd like to see Mrs

85

Daniel."

She removed her glasses and cleaned the lenses on the hem of her skirt. "I'm afraid we've no one of that name in this ward," she said.

"The lady in room 35," said Garnett.

"There's nobody in room 35, it's being redecorated."

"Have you got a key to the room?" said Markham.

"Of course, it's in my office."

Markham flashed his ID card again. "I'd like to borrow it please."

She slipped between them and went into her office leaving the door open while she checked the key board. Her finger hovered over a blank space and her face registered disbelief. "I don't understand it," she said, "the key is missing."

Garnett said, "Was it there when you came on duty, Sister?"

"I'm not sure," she said.

"We'll take a look anyway, perhaps the door isn't locked." She looked as though she was going to follow them until Garnett said, "Please don't bother to come with us, Sister, we've taken up too much of your time already."

She smiled gratefully. "Turn to your right," she said, "it's the fourth door on the left."

When they were out of earshot, Markham said; "We could be wasting our time. The odds are that she's been moved on."

"I thought I made it clear that nothing was to happen to her?"

"For fuck sake," Markham said irritably, "nothing has happened to her. We just had to move her to a safer place than this. Look, the registrar makes a room available when we need it. Usually it is one that is going to be redecorated, or something like that. Any excuse will do so long as the regular staff are kept away but the understanding is that we have our people in and out in less than twenty-four hours."

They stopped outside the room and Garnett tried the door. "It's locked," he said, "can you open it?"

"I've got a bunch of keys here that will open anything." He grinned at Garnett, and said, "I got this little lot off a villain I did for breaking and entering. "He turned the lock and opened the door on an empty room. "What did I tell you, she's in transit."

The room didn't look as if the decorators were in. The bed was still made up, but not to hospital standards. It just didn't look right to Garnett.

"Hey," said Markham, "the bedspread is damp." He got down on his hands and knees and peered under the bed. "There's several fragments of glass under here. What do you make of that?"

Garnett didn't answer him because he had the wardrobe open and the auburn haired woman with the muscular legs was staring up at him with a blank look in her eyes. She was lying on her side, wrists and ankles tied together behind her back with what appeared to be strips of pink nylon. A great wad of frothy pink nightdress had been stuffed into her mouth, and a streak of blood oozed from the puncture mark on her arm where the hypodermic needle had been forced in. Her hair was matted and the gag was stained a dark shade of brown in places. She was quite naked and he thought she was dead until he detected a faint pulse beat.

"Oh Christ," said Markham quietly, "is she all right?"

"Not too good, I think her skull could be fractured. Do you know who she is?"

"Oh aye. She's Brenda Jackson the physiotherapist. We used her because she had access to all the wards without drawing comment. There are times, you see, when you don't want the person in transit to know where they are going; you follow me?"

"You fill them up with dope."

"When it's necessary. She was probably about to give Stanton a shot of pentathol, and got hit over the head, most likely with the water jug. Leastways that would explain the broken glass and the damp bed cover. I don't suppose Stanton meant to hit her quite so hard, I mean why else did she use the shot of pentathol on Brenda?"

Garnett said, "We need to get her to a doctor."

"Yes," said Markham. "Hunt will have to know too, but I can fix that." He slammed the palm of his hand against the woodwork. "How much of a head start do you think she has on us?"

"What time is it?"

Markham checked his watch. "Eight-fifteen," he said.

"I left her at twelve."

"It could be as much as eight hours then. You wait for me in the car while I get this sorted out."

Garnett said okay. He left Women's Surgical and found a public call box in the entrance hall. He called Dane. In a roundabout way she told him London wasn't too happy about the situation. He said London could get stuffed.

10

Halliday was a quiet, reserved man. He was also a very brave one. As a nineteen year old National Serviceman he had won a DCM in Korea for knocking out a Chicom machine gun post single handed. In bald terms, the citation stated that Halliday was a member of a fighting patrol which had been sent across the Han River to take out a known enemy observation post on Point 694. The patrol subsequently discovered that the observation post was no longer occupied, and, on making their way back to their own lines, the patrol was ambushed and pinned to the ground by well directed machine gun fire from close range. With complete disregard for his own safety, Lance-Corporal Halliday had charged the enemy firing his Bren gun from the hip. Hit in the shoulder, left leg and right arm by grenade fragments, he nevertheless closed with the enemy and destroyed the machine gun post. It was perhaps typical of Halliday that very few of his associates knew anything of this action.

Most of his fellow police officers were, however, aware that some fourteen years later he attracted the attention of the Watch Committee as a result of alleged brutality. In this instance the record was there for all to see.

Halliday, by this time a Detective Constable, was assigned to keep watch on the Labour Day Anti-Vietnam Rally. In common with all other officers on duty that day, he had been specifically briefed to avoid provocation because it was said that the organisers of the protest rally were as keen as the police to avoid violence. Unfortunately their good intentions were lost on the rank and file of the demonstrators, a considerable body of whom broke away from the main procession and rampaged through the city streets, smashing the windows of local government offices and daubing slogans on public buildings. At four o'clock in the afternoon, some eight hours after he had come on duty, Halliday was directed, over the Panda Radio net, to investigate a reported disturbance in the area of the Union Building.

The disturbance involved four youths who were beating up one police constable. When Halliday arrived on the scene, three of them were holding the policeman while the fourth worked him over with his fists. He moved in behind the man who was doing the punching, spun him round and felled him with a forearm smash. Later it transpired that Halliday had fractured his jaw and the man spent the next two months in hospital with his jaw wired up and being fed through a drip. Of the remaining three, one charged head first intending to butt Halliday in the stomach, but instead made contact with a bony kneecap which broke his nose and cheek bones. Another, rushing forward, happened to trip over Halliday's outstretched leg and fell down a steep flight of steps, thereby breaking one ankle; and the fourth, intent on getting out of Halliday's way, ran into a lamp post and was still suffering from the after effects of concussion some twenty-four hours later. All four subsequently lodged a complaint which in the end turned out to be a somewhat futile exercise.

Halliday was a taciturn man by nature; the older men on the force, who could remember that far back, likened him to Gary Cooper, except that in comparison Cooper had been almost voluble. Tonight, however, Halliday was in a talkative mood.

"Wouldn't surprise me," he said, "if we weren't in for a warm spell. It might be unseasonable but it has happened in the past; March '67 or was in '68? Real scorcher. The signs are all there, cold snap followed by rain."

Garnett said, "I'm all for a change."

Halliday shifted in his seat. "Markham's a long time," he observed.

"He has a lot on his plate."

"You're right there. He thought a lot of Brenda Jackson, knew her for years he did."

"Oh yes?"

90

"Grew up together, went to the same school." He drummed his fingers on the steering wheel, "I think he was pretty keen on her at one time."

The door opened and Markham slid in beside Halliday. "Someone talking about me?" he said grimly.

"Only in the nicest possible way," said Garnett.

"All right, if we've finished gossiping perhaps we can go after the girl."

Halliday flicked the engine into life, shifted into gear, and said; "Okay, where do we start?"

"With Mrs Beckwith; ten to one that's where she went after she left the hospital. She would need to get rid of Jackson's uniform, get hold of some clothes and make contact with her husband."

"Tolcroft Road it is," said Halliday. He made a U turn and swept out of the car park. "Shall we let control know where we are?"

"Have they asked?"

"No."

"Then don't say anything until they request a location."

"Whatever you say," said Halliday.

The Militia had established a check point at the cross roads below Monkbar with a couple of Land-Rovers parked diagonally across the road in such a way that oncoming traffic was forced to negotiate a slow S Bend. A sentry flagged them down with a torch to indicate that they should pull into the side of the road. Halliday took no notice; blue light flashing and klaxon blaring, he went through the road block as if it wasn't there.

Markham whistled loudly. "You're pushing our luck," he said.

"They were too slow witted to think of opening fire."

"Next time we won't put it to the test, you hear me?"

"I hear you," said Halliday.

Markham relaxed and leaned back in the seat. He lit a cigarette and then said, "According to Hunt, Stanton was to be transferred to a private nursing home in Scarborough around four-thirty this afternoon. Jackson would have prepared her for the journey about thirty minutes beforehand and the curfew came on at seven. She had three hours therefore in which to get clear of the city."

"They could still be in York."

"I hope so."

Garnett said, "She had no money on her, so telephoning was out. It would take her over half an hour to reach Tolcroft Road from the hospital on foot. Fifteen minutes if she pinched a bicycle."

Halliday drove past Tolcroft Road and pulled into the forecourt of the Drum and Fife, dousing the car lights and ignition as he did so. The engine died reluctantly. The pub was in darkness. He opened his door and got out to make way for Garnett.

Halliday said, "Now's the time to find out how good a detective you are."

"You want me to question her?"

Halliday glanced at Markham. "That's the general idea," he said.

"And you're going to wait for me here?"

"That's right."

"Okay," said Garnett, "make sure you do."

As he walked away, Markham called out, "Keep your eyes open, we don't want you walking into a patrol."

He needn't have worried; there were no patrols in the vicinity of Tolcroft Road. The street was deserted, even the moggies were observing the curfew.

Garnett stopped outside number 49. The front of the house was in darkness. Upstairs, where the curtains had not been drawn, the reflection of the orange street lamps was mirrored in the windows. He pushed open the gate and walked quietly up the front path; breaking off a twig from the privet hedge as he went along. To the right of the door, and set into the wall, was a button marked push. He pressed the bell and jammed it with the twig. The bell was pealing insistently as he walked round the side of the house and opened the back gate.

Garnett picked up a stone, smashed the glass panel in the kitchen door, slipped his arm inside and turned the lock. He groped his way around inside the dark kitchen, skirted the breakfast table, opened another door and found himself in the hall. Beckwith was standing on the front doorstep, her back towards him.

"Hullo, there," he said quietly.

92

She jumped like a frightened cat and staggered back against the wall. Her left hand flew to her pumping heart and her jaw dropped. Garnett clapped his hand over her mouth before she had a chance to scream, and, using his free hand, groped round the door and removed the twig. The bell stopped ringing. He closed the door with his shoulder.

"We're not going to scream are we?" he said.

She shook her head vigorously and removed his hand from her mouth. There was a smell of peppermint on her breath.

"Where is everybody?" he said pleasantly.

"They've gone."

"All of them?"

"They walked out on me."

Garnett took hold of her arm. "Suppose we make sure?" He pushed her firmly towards the staircase. "You lead the way," he said.

There were four bedrooms off the first landing and another two above. Empty drawers lined with wax paper hung open in silent testimony to the hasty migration.

"You must have made yourself very popular."

She compressed her thin lips and looked down at the floor. She wasn't embarrassed, merely annoyed.

"They took just one man from this house," he continued, "and you told them where to find him because you didn't dare to take the risk of having the place searched from top to bottom. The lodgers must have loved you for that. Where was Stanton hiding?"

Her face took on a sullen expression. "In the loft behind the water tank," she said grudgingly.

"The house was too tidy," Garnett said absently, "usually when they have finished searching a house it looks as though it has been stripped by a hurricane. The penny should have dropped this morning."

"Have you seen all you want?"

"I think so, let's go downstairs and have a talk."

She wasn't very keen on the idea but she didn't have any option. She closed the bedroom doors and led the way downstairs to a

93

sitting room at the back of the house.

The furniture in the small back room was arranged around a twenty-three inch television set. A half empty bottle of gin, a sticky bottle of concentrated orange juice, a tumbler smeared with lipstick and a bag of peppermint sweets littered the small table beside the armchair. A black handbag lay on the floor.

"Been celebrating?"

She looked at him blankly.

"You've been knocking the gin."

"Medicinal," she said.

"How long has she been gone?"

"Who?"

"Your niece."

"She's not my niece, how many more times have I got to tell you?"

"Is that why you charged her four hundred pounds to stay here?"

"Four hundred?" Her voice went up an octave. "They haven't got that kind of money."

Garnett picked up her handbag and emptied the contents out on to the table, knocking the gin bottle on to the floor. The precious liquid began to spill out on to the Indian carpet. For a large woman, Beckwith could move surprisingly fast when the need to arose. She had the cap back on the bottle before much more than a tot was lost.

Garnett rifled through the contents of her handbag, discarding lipstick pencil, compact, purse, handkerchief, a bottle of smelling salts, eyebrow pencil, nail file, Biro, purse and diary before he found what he was looking for.

"See this?" He waved a book under her nose. "It's your clothing coupons. Next issue is due at the end of June, and you haven't any left because you gave them all to Stanton so that she could buy herself some clothes."

Beckwith got up from the floor where she had been grovelling on her hands and knees and poured a generous measure of gin into the tumbler which she topped up with orange juice. Garnett removed the glass from her hand when it was half way to her mouth.

"She may have killed a nurse," he said flatly.

"I don't believe you."

"You don't imagine she won those clothes in a raffle do you?"

"You're trying to make trouble for me."

Garnett placed his hand on her shoulder and pushed her down into the armchair. "I don't have to," he said, "you're doing all right on your own. Shaking the Stantons down for hush money and then laying the odds off with the city police. When did you phone them?"

She started to say "the day before yesterday," and then closed her mouth.

"And after you had taken them for four hundred. Oh no, I don't have to make trouble for you, Mrs Beckwith, you're already in it, way over your head; because now the danger is that Stanton is going to get himself picked up by the Russians, and if he talks to them, believe me nobody is going to lift a finger to help you. Your best hope is that I get to them first." He leaned forward over her and said, "Isn't it about time you started looking out for yourself again?"

Her eyes slid away from his and he knew she was going to lie for some reason which he couldn't begin to fathom.

She licked her lips and then said; "They talked of going to Eire and staying the night in Halifax before going on to Manchester tomorrow."

"Where in Halifax?"

"Let me see now." She snapped her fingers, "How stupid of me, it's slipped my mind: 175, no 178 Westbourne Drive, that's it, 178 Westbourne Drive."

"And the name of these people who are putting them up for the night?"

"Mr and Mrs Scott."

"When did they leave?"

"About a couple of hours ago," she said confidently.

"You're a liar, Mrs Beckwith," he said calmly. "It is now nine o'clock; the curfew came on at seven. They wouldn't chance their arm like that. Now just where the hell are they?"

"I honestly don't know."

Garnett didn't believe her but they both knew he wouldn't use force to prise the information out of her. As he stood up, his eyes lighted on four Dresden figures standing on the mantelpiece above the hearth. They were each about twelve inches high and at a very rough guess he thought they would fetch about a hundred and fifty. He picked up the largest figure, a shepherdess, and examined the marking in the base. "Very nice," he said, "fairly old, before the First World War. Family heirloom?"

"They belonged to my grandmother."

Her anxious tone of voice told him that she treasured them. Garnett opened his hand and let the figure fall into the fireplace. He picked up the ballerina and dropped it on to the decapitated shepherdess. His hand hovered above the milkmaid. "Where did you say they were hiding?" he said casually.

"For God's sake," she shouted, "they are at Peacock and Ives, it's a disused warehouse on the Foss Islands Road."

Garnett picked up the tumbler of gin and gave it to her. "Here," he said, "drink this, you've earned it."

She found it necessary to use both hands to hold the glass steady while she drank from it. Presently, she said, "What am I going to do?"

Garnett said; "Normally, I don't give advice but with you I'll make an exception. If I were in your shoes, Mrs Beckwith, I'd leave York and find somewhere else to live before my neighbours got too unpleasant. If you do decide to stay, buy yourself a wig against the time they shave the hair off your head." He walked out of the room and closed the door behind him.

The telephone was standing on a pile of women's magazines on the window shelf by the front door. Garnett paused long enough to rip out the earth terminal just in case Beckwith was tempted to make a call, and then, keeping a wary eye out for curfew patrols, he made his way back to the car.

Patience was a virtue unknown to Markham, and waiting drained what little reserves he had. At the sound of Garnett's footsteps, he flung open the car door and stepped out on to the forecourt. "What kept you?" he snarled.

Garnett ignored him. He climbed into the Viva and sat behind Halliday. Markham got back inside and slammed the door.

"Well?" he said.

"Well, what?"

"Did she cough?"

Garnett said, "They are supposed to be hiding out in Peacock and Ives. Do you know it?"

"It's an old warehouse on the Foss Islands Road. Do you think she was telling you the truth?"

"There's only one way to find out."

"All right," said Markham, "we'll take a look. If she is lying we'll come back and beat her ears off."

He sounded as though he meant it.

Halliday started the Viva and pulled off the forecourt of the Drum and Fife. He drove steadily, whistling a tuneless dirge through his teeth. A military policeman flashed by on a motorcycle and disappeared round the bend of the road, the blat of his exhaust fading in the distance. Seconds later, the exhaust note began to climb up the decibel range again and then the motorcyclist reappeared in view, coming towards them from the opposite direction. He went past them at sixty and never gave them a second glance.

"Show off," muttered Halliday.

The name was splashed across the front of the warehouse in black Gothic letters two feet high, and, at a casual glance, the building reminded Garnett of a chapel. The windows on the ground floor were boarded up haphazardly by one inch planks nailed together in criss cross fashion. Nobody had bothered to do anything about the windows in the floors above, but here and there a pane of glass still remained defiantly intact. Halliday pulled into the kerb a short distance beyond the warehouse.

"This should do us all right," he said quietly. "There's an alley about ten yards back which leads through to the rear entrance. Do you want me to come with you?"

Markham said, "We can handle it, you stay with the car."

97

He opened the door and got out. Garnett joined him on the pavement. A powerful headlight suddenly pierced the darkness at the top of the street and came towards them. As the vehicle drew closer they saw that it was a riot proof Land-Rover. Two militiamen in olive drab combat suits and baseball caps sat up front; behind them, a couple of wooden faced Russians hugged Kalashnikov assault rifles to their chests. The patrol veered towards them as if drawn by a magnet.

"That's all we needed," Markham whispered.

An officer got out leisurely. He was a small man but his arrogant bearing made up for his lack of inches. His face reminded Garnett of a ferret. He had all the necessary qualifications to be a first class four letter man.

"What's going on?" He tried to sound pleasant and friendly but the nasal inflection of his voice never failed to put peoples' backs up.

Nobody said a word in reply. Markham cleared his throat and shifted his feet like a small boy caught lying. A falsely refined voice broke the silence on the police net to ask their location, and Halliday thankfully answered the call.

"I'm waiting for an answer."

The tone was cold and demanding. Garnett felt as though he had been reprimanded. One of us should say something, he thought, before this cretin decides to really throw his weight around.

Garnett said, "We think two curfew breakers hopped inside that warehouse when they saw our headlights."

"What's the problem then?"

"There is no problem, Lieutenant."

"Captain."

"I'm sorry," Garnett said politely, "I'm not familiar with Army ranks. Now that you are here, perhaps you wouldn't mind watching the front of the building while we go in at the back?"

"I think we could do that for you. I didn't catch your name?"

"Daniel, sir, Detective Sergeant Daniel. This is Detective Constable Markham, Detective Constable Halliday behind the wheel."

The "sir," went down well. The captain even managed to draw himself up another inch. "Right," he said pompously, "let's get

98

started."

"What about the Ivans?"

The taller of the two Russians glared at Garnett. "Shut your goddam lip, you Limey creep," he bawled. The American accent sounded ludicrous coming out of a Mongolian face.

The captain shrank a little and looked almost humble. "I should watch your step if I were you, Sergeant Daniel," he said, and then, in a voice which definitely was pleading, added, "I suggest we get on with the job in hand."

Garnett said; "You're quite right, sir." He turned to Halliday and said, "You stay here and keep control posted, while Markham and I take a look."

They walked away as quickly as they could without appearing to be in an indecent haste, conscious that the obnoxious militia captain was staring at them hard, as if he was trying to remember them for future reference.

The narrow cobbled alley stank of urine. What was left of a pair of swing gates afforded entrance into the back yard of Peacock and Ives. Grass, weeds, and saplings sprouted through the cracks in the concrete. Broken glass and a multitude of rusty tin cans forced them to move slowly and carefully in order not to make a noise.

"We're going to have trouble with that captain," Markham whispered. "He took the number of our patrol car, and you can bet he is going to ask around after a Detective Sergeant Daniel."

"Perhaps he won't be able to ask any awkward questions."

"What's that supposed to mean?"

Garnett touched Markham's arm and drew him into the shadow of the wall. A rat scuttled across the yard and disappeared behind a pile of rubbish. A door creaked in the faint breeze.

"There was a movement up there on the third floor. I think they have seen us."

Markham said; "You must have infra red eyes."

"You take it from me, they are there all right." He paused and then whispered; "Do you know what a fire fight is?"

"No, should I?"

"Not really. Sometimes a soldier can get jumpy and start shooting

99

at what he thinks is the enemy. When it is a dark night, the eyes can play funny tricks. Of course nine times out of ten nothing is there, but once in a while it is one of our own incoming patrols, and they start shooting back and then you've got yourself a fire fight."

"So, where does that get us?"

Garnett slipped the Remington out of the shoulder holster and thumbed the hammer back. "So I am going to fire on the patrol, and you are going to stay here and fix the Stantons when they come running out, and if you make it look good, we might even get those hostages released."

There was an audible click, a rushing noise not unlike someone breathing heavily and then a plummy voice boomed through a loud hailer, the speech distorted beyond recognition as the sound bounced off the warehouse.

Garnett said; "The captain is getting impatient. Now remember, when they come running out, you start shooting."

Keeping close to the wall, Garnett inched his way towards the fire escape on the left side of the building. He paused to listen at the foot of the iron ladder, and hearing nothing, bounded quickly up to the first floor, and slipped in through an open window. As he waited to allow his eyes to adjust to the gloom, a spotlight from the Land-Rover flicked across the front of the warehouse, the beam striking the ceiling and silhouetting a dozen or so giant packing crates which were scattered haphazardly around the floor. The plummy voice started broadcasting again, masking the sound of his footsteps on the wooden staircase which led to the floor above.

Garnett worked his way over to a window which looked out on to the street below. The captain was standing by the Land-Rover, the battery powered megaphone held loosely in his right hand. The driver stood beside him directing the spot up at the building while the two Russians were on the canal side of the street some twenty metres apart.

He brought the Remington up double handed, the left hand grasping the right wrist to support it. He squeezed off two shots in quick succession when the foresight niche lined up on the captain's stomach. The baseball cap flew up in the air as the .45 pulped into

100

his head. Traversing quickly, Garnett fired on the nearest Russian before ducking back out of sight. A spray of automatic fire chipped the brickwork around the window frame above his head.

Garnett crawled out of the line of fire and, when he thought it was safe enough, he rushed the stairs to the floor above. As he emerged on the third floor a door banged at the far end of the long room and he could briefly hear their footsteps on the iron rungs of the other fire escape. He moved to the nearest window and took another pot shot at the Land-Rover. The spot light went out abruptly. In between the bursts of gunfire he thought he heard somebody scream.

Garnett worked his way down to the ground floor and cautiously stepped out into the backyard. He saw them immediately. They were lying a mere five metres apart; each one curled up like a foetus in the womb. They looked small and ugly in death.

Markham moved towards him, a wooden expression on his face. In a dull voice, he said; "He stood quite still when he saw me, just stood there pissing himself. He didn't have a gun, he didn't do anything, he just stood there and waited for me to shoot him and then she screamed."

Garnett held out the Remington, butt first. "You'd better plant this on him. Did you remember to bring a .22 target pistol?"

"It's in the car."

"Make sure you plant that on him as well, if you get the chance."

"What are you going to do?"

"Hide up somewhere until morning when it will be safe to move."

"Okay," said Markham, "I'll go and stop the war."

He turned away from Garnett and walked out of the yard. One of the Ivans was still hammering away with his Kalashnikov.

11

The alarm woke Garnett. Yawning loudly, he propped himself up in the bed and rubbed his eyes. Dust motes danced in the beam of light cast through the window by the late afternoon sun. He yawned again, threw the blankets off and sat on the edge of the bed while he collected his wits. He was still sitting there when Dane entered the room.

"You're up," she said brightly.

"I'm up," he agreed.

"London called, they want us to return on the five forty-one."

He reached for the packet of cigarettes lying on the bedside table and took one. "Did they give any reason why they wanted us back?"

She shook her head. "They couldn't tell me very much."

"Couldn't or wouldn't?"

"I don't know."

"Have you heard how Markham and Halliday made out after I left them?"

"I haven't been in touch with Hunt."

"You're a mine of information," he said. He lit the cigarette and inhaled. "I don't suppose Coleman has anything to do with London wanting us back, has he?"

"I don't think so. What have you got against Coleman?"

"He wants me dead."

He could see disbelief register in her face as she sank down into a chair. Her tongue flicked out and moistened her lips.

"What on earth has got into you," she said huskily. "Are you feeling all right?"

"I am not going round the bend if that is what you are thinking. Do you want to hear about it?"

102

"I think I'd better."

He leaned forward towards her and said; "It started eighteen months ago when we began to lose a lot of our people in District 7. The cells involved were centred on Harrow, Kenton and Wealdstone. It was pretty clear to us that MI 5 had recruited some double agents. We had to know their names and fortunately we had Endicott who was in a position to get them for us. When we got the list of informers, Coleman had them executed. It wasn't very clever because we had as good as disclosed our source of information, and for some weeks Endicott was walking on thin ice. He never forgave us."

Garnett stubbed the cigarette out in the glass ashtray on the bedside table. "We left Endicott pretty much alone after that, but when the Pollard affair broke, we put the bite on him again. I think it must have come as a nasty shock and he made up his mind to break with us once and for all. Endicott had never met Coleman, but he knew me well enough and my guess is that he decided to use me as a means of taking the pressure off himself. He got some of his people to involve me in a brawl which gave him the excuse to arrest me. I was charged with causing a breach of the peace, fingerprinted and fined. He then served notice on Coleman that he meant business by having me shadowed."

Garnett stood up and walked over to the washbasin and ran the hot water tap. "The Stantons came up here because they thought they would be safe. What they didn't know was that Hunt and his friends had the whole town very much where they wanted it. Beckwith knew from the news broadcast that the police were after the Stantons and so she told Hunt she had them under her roof. At that stage, Hunt wasn't aware that the Stantons were also running away from the Resistance."

He dropped the plug into the basin and began to lather the shaving brush. "Coleman got my letter the next morning, and started checking the list of possible contacts. He sent you up to York and got in touch with Hunt and that's when he heard that Hunt already knew where the Stantons were hiding. About the same time Coleman also became aware that Endicott was going to put the

103

squeeze on him."

Garnett lathered his face and began to shave carefully. "So he thought up a neat way of solving all his problems in one foul swoop. He got in touch with Hunt again and arranged a simple but effective plan. I was to fix the Stantons and then I would be shot down."

"You must be mistaken," Dane said firmly. "This isn't a jungle. Our people simply wouldn't behave like that." She gesticulated wildly. "I just don't believe it. It's too incredible."

Garnett put the razor to one side, rinsed his face and then dried it on a hand towel. "I don't think it is," he said. "I arrived at eight-fifty the day before yesterday, and, of all the passengers who got out at York, I was the only one to be stopped by the police. Why? Because Halliday and Markham had been told that I would arrive on that train and they had a general description of me, and they wanted a close look so that they would have no trouble in recognising me again. I was told where to find the Stantons and was given a cannon for the job, but that is all the help I did get. After I had shot them, I was supposed to walk six hundred metres to the car and a lot can happen in six hundred metres. I think Halliday and Markham would have been waiting for me outside if those two Russians hadn't been killed, and but for them I wouldn't be here now."

"For God's sake," Dane said hoarsely, "and what part do you think I am supposed to have played in all this?"

Garnett finished wiping the razor clean and put it away in the washbag. "You didn't fit into the plan at all. Coleman sent you up here before he got in touch with Hunt. Having sent you up here, Coleman was obliged to string you along so they used you to relay orders to me. As far as you were concerned there had been no change of plan."

"If," she said slowly, "if you believe all this to be true, why are you going back?"

"Because there is nowhere else I can go."

Dane stood up. "I hope you know what you are doing," she said, "if I were in your place, I wouldn't go anywhere near London." She shrugged her shoulders, "But then I'm not in your shoes. I'll go and get you something to eat. You must be starving."

Garnett finished dressing, packed his things and then went into the kitchen. Dane had cooked eggs and bacon, but despite being hungry, he ate slowly and merely picked at the food. No matter how he tried, he couldn't push the Stantons out of his mind.

It had been a mistake on somebody's part to recruit them in the first place, and for Pollard to use them on a job which entailed a total disregard for human life was an error of judgment which passed all understanding. Yet no allowance had been made for their failure, and they had been executed without compunction. Whichever way he looked at it, the part he had played in the affair sickened him. He pushed the plate to one side and drank the cup of tea.

Dane cleared the breakfast things away and stacked the crockery in the sink. "I don't want to hurry you," she said, "but if we want to make sure of a seat on the train, we should think about leaving."

"Of course," he said absently, "I'll get the bags."

Halliday had been right about the weather. It was hard to realise that even spring had not yet arrived. Apart from the naked branches on the trees, it was hot enough to be taken for a summer's evening. It would have been a good time to relax in a garden chair with a long cool drink and a good woman near at hand. Well, he had a good woman near at hand, but he was sitting on the top deck of a bus instead of being out on the lawn and he certainly didn't have a long cool drink.

They need not have hurried. There was no great rush for the five forty-one, and he had time enough in which to get an evening paper before finding an empty compartment next to the guard's van.

He put the bags up in the rack, and then sat down in a corner seat by the corridor and opened his copy of the *West Riding Evening Post*. Splashed across the front page was a photograph of a group of men taken outside the barracks as they emerged through the gates. A number of them smiled nervously into the camera, a few even looked apologetic. The caption simply said, "Released." The names of the twenty men who had been executed as an example to the others appeared at the foot of the page edged in black.

He looked to see what the paper had to say about the Stantons.

They merited a small column on page two with the inference that the police were satisfied that they had been responsible for the killing of the two Russians. It sounded pretty thin. There was no mention of Halliday or Markham.

The well modulated voice of the station announcer intoned details of the train's schedule over the tannoy. A whistle shrilled, and the carriage jerked as their airbrakes were unlocked and the diesel began to take up the haul. Slowly, the train began to edge its way out of the platform.

At the last minute, the door swung open; a grip sailed through the air and landed at Garnett's feet. The grip was followed by a slightly built militia officer who ended up on his hands and knees. A porter slammed the door shut behind him.

The officer got up, brushed the dust off his uniform, picked up the grip and placed it in the rack above Garnett's head. He removed his cap, smoothed his hair back in place with the palms of both hands and then sat down. His eyes met Garnett's over the top of the paper, and his face gradually broke into a thin lipped smile.

"Well, this is a surprise," he said, "It is David Seymour, isn't it?"

Dane looked up from her magazine, caught the warning look in Garnett's eye and lowered her head again.

Garnett said; "Hullo, Lethbridge, fancy meeting you again." He tried not to make it sound as if the end of the world had come.

"Well, well," said Lethbridge. He shook his head in amazement. "I can't get over it. How long is it since we last saw one another? Four years? The Lichfield Detention Centre." He leaned forward and placed a well manicured hand on Garnett's knee. "When did they release you?"

He sounded like a woman with her lover. Fighting back a feeling of revulsion Garnett said; "Just over three years ago."

"A little before me. I can't tell you how pleased I am to see you again, David." The hand squeezed his knee warmly. "You had a very rough time. Did you find Elizabeth."

Oh you bastard, Garnett thought, you know bloody well I didn't. Aloud, he said, "She was killed."

"I'm extremely sorry."

106

It was said without feeling and he didn't mean it. Looking at his long pointed face, and perpetually sneering thick lips, Garnett wondered, not for the first time, how he had avoided being beaten up while he was incarcerated in the prison camp. He had the happy knack of getting people's backs up, except of course those that mattered.

"What are you doing with yourself now?" said Lethbridge.

"I'm with Axel Insurance."

"I thought you had ideas about the law?"

"I failed to qualify."

"You should have stayed in the Army. You were a good soldier, I've always thought so from the day we met. You remember that day?"

Oh, he remembered all right. Garnett would never forget that day. Mid August, and the corn should have been standing high and golden in the warm sunlight, but instead the crops were burning. The village was burning, and so were the trucks and so too were some of the soldiers. And above them, indifferent to the destruction they had wrought, the flight of FARMER ground attack planes climbed gracefully in the clear sky and set course for home and lemon tea, or whatever it was the Ivans favoured at the end of a mission. Lethbridge arrived in the middle of this mess of charred bodies looking absurdly smart and out of place. If he had said one wrong word or made some flippant remark that day, he would have had his head beaten in. He did no such thing. Quietly and methodically he set about patching up the wounded. At a time when Garnett had lost control, he restored order. It is easy to hate someone who has no redeeming features; the trouble with Lethbridge was that he had too many.

Garnett said, "You saved our bacon that day."

"I was looking for Brigade headquarters. I never did find them."

The world that summer seemed to be populated with confused and disoriented men; stragglers looking for their parent unit, and units out of touch with Formation Headquarters and acting on their own initiative because there was a widespread feeling that no one was attempting to control events.

107

They stumbled across the helicopter landing zone shortly after the air attack. They were hiding up in a copse while they tried to establish radio contact with the battalion. Below the copse, a patchwork of cornfields and lush green pastures separated by neat hedgerows stretched as far as the eye could see. In the middle distance, a woman in a blue dress was riding a bicycle along the lane which led to a farmhouse half hidden by a fold in the ground. Only a faint threshing sound disturbed the peace and quiet; the war could have been a million light years away, and then quite suddenly it wasn't so far away after all.

The woman did not look up as the Hound helicopter came in low out of the sun and hovered over the area. Puffs of white dust spurted up along the lane and the woman wobbled from side to side on the bicycle before falling off into the ditch. For a brief second, the scene reminded Garnett of an excerpt from an old Mack Sennet comedy which he had seen on television and then the chattering roar of the machine guns shattered the illusion.

Like vultures, a cluster of troop carriers waddled up and disgorged their load in anxious haste. They soared upwards leaving behind them a hundred and fifty paratroops trying to get into some sort of order. It was a golden opportunity, a once in a lifetime turkey shoot and nobody waited for orders. A fox inside a battery layer could not have caused greater panic. Like decapitated hens, the paratroopers ran about in wild circles, their limbs jerking spastic-like as one by one they were shot down. A few made for the shelter of a corn field where the 81mm. mortars reached out and cremated them in a sea of white phosphorous. They were still shooting when there was nothing left alive to shoot at, and stopping them was the hardest thing Garnett did that day.

Lethbridge produced a gun metal cigarette case from the inside pocket of his jacket. He flipped it open and offered Garnett a cigarette.

"Recognise it? Of course you do. Corporal Wyngarde gave it to me just before he died of pneumonia."

Garnett leaned forward and took a light from Lethbridge's lighter. He tried to recall what Wyngarde looked like and remembered a rather pale faced, fair haired man the other prisoners referred to as Lucy, because young as he was, he was a bit of an old woman. He was forever sweeping the area around his bunk like a fussy houseproud woman.

"We were lucky to survive considering what the conditions were like in that camp," Lethbridge said casually.

The conversation was taking a dangerous turn. Garnett wanted to avoid the subject of prison camps in case Lethbridge started to ask some awkward questions. In a very short time they would be drawing into Grantham, and he made up his mind that he would leave the train there, and in the meantime he had to change the topic of conversation somehow. Almost desperately, he cast about in his mind for something original to say. When at last he spoke up, his words were trite.

Garnett said, "We certainly gave the Ivans a run for their money."

Lethbridge flicked the ash from his cigarette on to the strip of carpet. He studied the glowing tip as if seeking inspiration. "What a curious expression," he said. "We gave them a run for their money. They beat us. The Deterrent failed and they beat us. It was as simple as that. We had an arsenal of terrifying weapons which we couldn't and didn't dare to use. But they did. Just the one, to show us that it was all over, and that's the way our world ended, not with a whimper but with a bang."

The train clattered across the points, swayed and then steadied to a rhythmical see saw. There was a long drawn out wooshing sound as they swept through a tiny wayside station. Garnett didn't catch its name.

Lethbridge cleared his throat and said; "If it hadn't been for you, I wouldn't be alive today. You gave me good advice. Remember? You suggested we removed our badges of rank before we surrendered so that we could pass as private soldiers. I'm glad I followed your advice. Even now I can still see those poor devils who went into the bag as officers, sitting cross legged on the rifle range, blindfolded, hands tied behind their backs, and a white card hung over their heart as an aiming mark."

He knew Lethbridge had a purpose. This just wasn't idle talk. In

109

his own good time, he would come to the point. Garnett just hoped they would slide into Grantham before he made it. Aloud, he said, "I helped to bury them."

"So did I, old boy, behind the stop butts in an open trench filled with quicklime. Believe me, after seeing that, I took my hat off to you when you went over the wall. That really took courage."

"I had a reason."

"Of course," said Lethbridge, "you had to find out what had happened to your wife."

Lethbridge brushed a speck of ash off his trousers and inspected the immaculately polished Sam Browne and pistol holster to see if it had been marked. The train was beginning to slow down for Grantham.

Garnett said, "Where are you stationed now?" He wasn't really interested, but he felt the need to say something to break the awkward silence."

Lethbridge looked up sharply. The expression on his face indicated that Garnett should not have asked. "York," he said tersely, "Karl Marx Barracks."

Against his better judgment Garnett said; "In the Intelligence Corps or shouldn't I ask?"

"Well, between old friends, I'm in Counter Intelligence."

"That must be interesting."

"Oh it is, we're beginning to get on top of these people."

"Who do you mean?" Garnett tried to sound casual and disinterested but to his own ears he sounded a shade too anxious.

"The Resistance."

His face was blank but Garnett sensed he was being pushed into a corner. He turned and stubbed his cigarette out in the ashtray by the sliding door, for the express purpose of seeing Dane's reaction. Outwardly she appeared to be concentrating on her magazine and giving the impression she was not listening to their conversation which was all to the good. He turned to face Lethbridge once more.

"I imagine," he said carefully, "you must be close to a breakthrough. It seems to me that, taking the country as a whole, the Resistance does not enjoy much support. I expect you get a lot of help from the public?"

"Not as much as we would like."

The train pulled into the station and slowed to a halt. A porter on the platform shouted, "Grantham, change here for Peterborough, Hitchin, and Welwyn Garden City.

Garnett smiled warmly. "I get off here," he said. "I must say it has been a pleasure meeting you again, Alan. We must keep in touch, perhaps we can get together for dinner one night, and talk over old times."

He stood up and reached for his briefcase and grip in the luggage rack.

Lethbridge said, "Please sit down, David, you're not going anywhere."

12

Garnett turned round. Lethbridge had moved so that he was out of reach. The Makarov 9mm. pistol in his hand was pointing at the centre of Garnett's chest.

"I'll shoot if I have to," he said.

Garnett sat down.

"You had better sit next to David, young woman, where I can keep my eye on you."

Dane looked up from her magazine, a surprised expression in her eyes. "I'm sorry," she said, "were you talking to me, by any chance?"

"There is only the three of us in the compartment, isn't there?" Lethbridge said coolly.

Dane said; "I'm afraid you are making a mistake, this gentleman and I are not acquainted. I've never seen him before."

"You're an awful liar. I saw him tip you the wink when I got into the compartment. So, please, no more play acting."

"You'd better do as he says," said Garnett.

"Now that's what I call a very sensible attitude."

Without a word, Dane picked up her handbag and sat down next to Garnett. She avoided looking at him and he could sense her disgust, but at that moment he didn't very much care what she thought of him. He was measuring the distance between himself and Lethbridge and the results of his calculation were hardly auspicious. Any move on his part and Lethbridge would kill him before he was half way out of his seat, unless of course there was a distraction. He glanced hopefully towards the platform, willing somebody to get into the compartment, but nobody, it seemed, wanted to ride in the last carriage.

The guard blew his whistle and the train started to draw out of the station. It struck him as being odd that Lethbridge had not taken them off the train and handed them over to the police, as he would have done had he been in Lethbridge's shoes. Perhaps he wasn't certain what to do with them, or maybe there was even the possibility that Lethbridge still felt obligated and didn't relish the idea of handing him over for certain execution.

"What do you plan to do with us?" he said.

Lethbridge considered the problem. "That's a good question," he said at last. "To tell you the truth, I haven't really made my mind up yet. I'm faced with a difficult decision because I feel I owe you a lot. Perhaps I am being sentimental."

"I'm in favour of that."

Lethbridge permitted himself a faint smile. "One good turn deserves another," he said vaguely.

"So the saying goes."

"Just think, if we hadn't run into one another again, you would probably have got away with it."

"Got away with what?"

"Don't you ever give up? I must be the one man in the Army who knows you were not released from detention and also knows you by sight. You are unique, David. You are the only man to have escaped from Parkhurst Military Prison. They sent you there after you had twice escaped from Lichfield, and by God you did it a third time. What a smack in the eye for the Ivans."

"Three cheers for me," said Garnett.

"Oh, I would cheer all right, if I wasn't so damn certain you were in the Resistance, and that, my dear chap, is precisely my problem. You see if I was convinced you had no connection with them, I'd let you both go without hesitation, but knowing you, there isn't a chance of that."

Garnett decided it was simply a time and motion problem. Somehow he had to get close to Lethbridge without alarming him, and then he would have to kill him and get rid of the body before the ticket collector poked his head into the compartment which ought to be shortly before they pulled into Kings Cross. He tried to

113

remember if anyone might have seen Lethbridge in the compartment with them, but he could not recall anyone passing by in the corridor.

Lethbridge said, "You're very quiet."

"You're holding the cards. It seems rather pointless to deny anything."

"You always were an honest man. You should have stayed in the Army where you belonged."

Garnett raised one eyebrow. "Somehow," he said, "I can't quite see myself as a Russian lackey."

Lethbridge flushed angrily. "We are not the servants of Moscow as you people like to make out. The trouble with your sort, David, is that you only know one way to skin a cat. Your way will merely ensure that the Russians stay on our backs forever. We have to pull the wool over their eyes. When they are convinced of our loyalty to Moscow, the occupation forces will be withdrawn and then we can start leading our own lives. When that happens we will need an Army to prevent them coming back again."

He was quite certain now that, providing he kept Lethbridge talking, he could close the gap between them an inch at a time. Getting rid of his body would be awkward. They couldn't leave it in the compartment and if they pushed it out on to the tracks too soon, it might be discovered before they reached Kings Cross.

Garnett said, "You didn't always feel this way. That time when we were both on an outside working party lifting potatoes, remember? You covered for me when I slipped away. And then when I went over the wall, you were the one who helped me to fix the door to our hut so that it was possible to lift it off its hinges when we were locked in for the night. And you were the one who organised our measures to combat the brain washing sessions."

Lethbridge smiled bitterly. "And I was the one they took out and stripped naked and lashed to a wooden horse for two days and nights with a twenty pound weight attached to each leg."

"Well, then," said Garnett, "you see you haven't really changed at all."

"Oh, but I have. I see things in a different light to you. I'm working for a better society."

114

"You mean you're working for a muzzled press and radio and the State controlling every aspect of our existence."

"And you're just mouthing claptrap. Over the years we've come to accept more and more State control. Before the war, we were, all of us, ever demanding that the government should do something about wildcat strikes, about the price of land, about bad landlords and a hundred and one other problem areas."

"And before the war," said Garnett, stealing another inch closer to Lethbridge, "you could stand up in public and tell everyone you thought the government stank. Try that today and see where it would get you."

"A lot of people would settle for stable prices, full employment, law and order, and security in their old age. Only the young have an affinity with the pavements; as you get older you realise that the only thing you get out of a protest movement is piles. And who knows, perhaps in time people will be allowed to criticise the government."

Dane said; "Is it all right if I smoke?" She opened her handbag and rummaged inside without waiting for Lethbridge to give his consent.

Lethbridge said; "Don't you ever do that again, you hear me? Next time I will shoot."

"I only want a cigarette, there's no need to make a drama out of it."

"You wait for my permission in future. Now bring your hand out of the bag slowly."

Dane withdrew her hand and opened it. "See," she said, "it's only a packet of cigarettes and a book of matches. Is it all right if I strike a match?"

Garnett didn't know what she had in mind, but as Dane didn't smoke he knew she had some plan in mind. To distract Lethbridge he said, "My trouble is that I am too old to change my spots."

Lethbridge glanced his way. "That's your bad luck," he said tersely.

Dane put the cigarette in her lips, struck a match, and then, without warning, bit through the filter tip and crushed it between

115

her teeth. The cigarette fell on to her lap, her legs began to shake uncontrollably and jack-knifing at the waist she pitched forward on to the floor.

Lethbridge said, "Christ, she's taken poison."

Without thinking he moved towards Dane and Garnett swung the edge of his palm across his wrist and broke it. The Makarov 9mm. dropped on to the floor and Garnett kicked it under the seat. He tried for a Bear, getting the heel of his palm under the nose and hooking for the eyes but Lethbridge caught him first with a forearm smash under the breastbone.

The force of the blow knocked him back against the seat and he fell over on to his back. Before he had a chance to recover, Lethbridge was on top of him, and using the left arm as a fulcrum across Garnett's throat, he tried to reach up for the communication cord with his damaged hand.

The blood was pounding in Garnett's ears and the light in the roof seemed to be drawing away. He got both hands under Lethbridge's chin and slowly forced his head back, relaxing the intolerable pressure on this throat. He had a vague recollection of the diesel locomotive howling like a demented banshee, and then the carriage was buffeted as an express passed them on the Up line. Lethbridge found the gap between his legs, and, thrusting a bony knee into the groin, sought to crush his testicles. The pain made him want to spew, and, Garnett, relaxing his hold, felt the full weight of the fulcrum arm back on his throat again.

The diesel shrieked again as they entered a long tunnel. There was a snapping noise not unlike the splintering of matchwood, and suddenly the pressure on his throat ceased and the blood was beginning to trickle out of Lethbridge's mouth. Garnett pushed the body on to the floor and sat up hugging his groin.

Dane looked down at the pistol in her hand and then said, "Are you all right?"

He nodded, caught his breath and said; "You're one hell of a fine actress. You could have fooled me, but if there is a next time, I'd appreciate it if you used the pistol a little sooner. You'd better close the blinds, we don't want anyone looking in on us."

116

He got to his feet slowly and opened the carriage window, and poked his head out into the tunnel. There was a patch of light not too far ahead which puzzled him for a moment until it dawned on him that they were coming out of the tunnel. The draught made his eyes water. A split second or so later they were running in the open country.

Garnett withdrew his head, turned to Dane and said; "We will have to shove him out of the window. Can you manage his legs?"

"I think so."

"All right, let's get it over and done with. Lift when I say ready."

It wasn't an easy job. His polished riding boots caught the top of the door and momentarily he hung, head down, suspended in space, until Garnett freed his toes and he dropped out of sight on to the track. Garnett picked up his Service dress hat and flung it out after him and then closed the window.

Dane said, "You've forgotten the grip and the pistol."

Garnett picked up the Makarov and wrapped it inside his handkerchief which he used like a shammy cloth to get the butt clean. Opening the window again, he tossed the pistol clear, and then grabbing hold of the grip he heaved it out. The grip bounced once and then rolled down the embankment. Garnett closed the window.

He turned to find Dane scuffing the carpet with the sole of her shoe. "I can't get it out," she said wildly.

"What?"

"The bloodstains."

He looked down and saw a number of dark brown spots. Stooping, and pushing Dane to one side, he flipped the haircord over on to its reverse side and trod it flat. "Nobody is going to notice that," he said confidently.

Her hands flew to her mouth. "The ticket collector," she said in a strangled voice, "he boarded the train at Grantham."

"I didn't see him."

"You were too busy watching the platform. He got on lower down the train and used the corridor to get to the guard's van."

"Did he look our way?"

"I don't know, he might have done. I only caught a glimpse of

117

him out of the corner of my eye. He could have seen Lethbridge. My God," she whispered, "what are we going to do?"

"We are going to keep calm." He put his hands on her shoulders and forced her to sit down. "If we keep our heads we will be all right. We'll give him something else to think about."

"Such as?"

"I'll think of something."

The train flashed through Hitchen.

"You'd better think of something quick." she said.

The ticket collector tipped the dregs of his tea out of the window and handed the chipped mug to the guard. He took the gold Hunter out of his waistcoat pocket and checked the time. It was part of his routine and the guard, waiting for his predictable comment which always followed this ritual, was not disappointed. "Time for my rounds," he said, "I wonder how many dodgers I'll catch in the lavatories tonight."

He winked at the guard and opened the door to the last carriage. As a matter of habit, he checked the lavatory first and then opened the door of the end compartment.

The couple hastily broke apart. The girl was a good looking bird with blonde hair and she was embarrassed when he stared at her. Her skirt and white slip were peeled back over her thighs and bunched up around her waist. She went crimson and struggled awkwardly to make herself look decent.

He scarcely noticed the man with her, although it did briefly occur to him that he was old enough to know better. He clucked his tongue wondering if he should voice his disapproval and decided against it. Absentmindedly he took the tickets from the man and backed out of the compartment still eyeing the girl. He thought it would make a good story to tell in the canteen when they reached Kings Cross; it also occurred to him it would have made an even better one if he had arrived five minutes later and caught them on the job.

13

They walked briskly along the platform towards the exit, mingling with the other passengers who had just got off the train. The passengers were passing freely through the gate which was a relief because if Lethbridge's body had been found, the police would have been screening everyone on the train. As they drew nearer the exit, a porter fell into step beside them and took the luggage off Garnett.

Out of the corner of his mouth, Robinson said; "Glad to see you back, Mr Garnett, we've been expecting you."

They were playing a Jim Reeves recording of Moon River at full blast over the tannoy and Garnett found it difficult to hear what Robinson said.

Still speaking softly, Robinson said, "You are to separate at the taxi rank. Miss Dane goes back to her place while you take a cab to 165 Havelock Gardens. You want flat number three, it belongs to Jean Inglis. You tell her Rollo sent you, she'll understand."

"Suppose I don't like the idea?"

Robinson flagged down a cab, placed his grip on the step next to the driver and ushered Garnett into the back. "You'll like it all right, man," he said with a broad grin.

The cab driver said, "Where to?"

Garnett said, "165 Havelock Gardens."

He caught a final glimpse of Dane standing dejectedly at the taxi rank with Robinson at her side. She seemed to tower over the small West Indian.

Havelock Gardens was a seedy looking square populated by poor whites, Pakistanis and West Indians. Terraced houses with slate roofs and peeling, grey-white distempered walls encircled a small park littered with rubbish and uprooted bushes. Garnett paid off the taxi

119

outside number 165 and then checked the list of names in the porch to make certain he had the right place. Jean Inglis described herself as a model. There were two other models on the premises, one called Pauline and the other Cathy. They all invited callers to walk upstairs. He pushed open the door and went inside.

A radio was playing somewhere in the house and the air reeked of boiled cabbage, curry and sour sweat. The staircase creaked under his weight, and, in the poor light, he tripped over the scuffed linoleum on the first floor landing. A dog started barking and then yelped when someone kicked it. He found himself staring at a plain card pinned on the chocolate brown door which instructed him to ring the bell. He did as he was asked. The door opened slowly.

Ash blonde hair framed a narrow face, small dark eyes watched him carefully. Tangerine sized breasts lurked behind a black bra, matching panties trimmed with red satin bows in the lace of the leg hugged a flat belly; net stockings and high heeled shoes emphasised legs which were too thin. A silver bracelet of good luck charms was fastened round one ankle.

"You have an appointment?" she said in a voice as husky as she could make it.

"Rollo sent me."

The warm smile faded. She stood to one side to let him enter and then closed the door behind him. "Your nine bob note is in the next room," she said. "You'd best follow me."

He noticed a crumpled bed, a stocking hanging out of a drawer in the dressing table, a box of Kleenex and a blue gym slip and leather strap draped over the back of a chair. She stopped by the door leading to the other room leaned against the wall and faced him.

"In there," she said. The saccharine smile appeared again. "Hope I don't disturb you. Remember me, if you should get bored with your friend."

Garnett opened the door and went into the room.

The man was standing by the window smoking a cigarette from a long black holder. Even in profile there was no mistaking the sad, bloodhound face and silver hair. He marvelled that Vickers, a member of the Army Board pre-war, had managed to avoid arrest for so long.

Garnett said, "This is a surprise, do I call you General?"

The eyes glinted in amusement. "It's not obligatory in these circumstances, Garnett."

"How do you know my name?"

"I'm well briefed, does that answer your question?"

"Not really."

"Let's just agree that I happen to know all about you. Please sit down."

"Am I in for a lecture?"

"An informal briefing."

Garnett raised an eyebrow. "Do you think this place is safe?"

"I imagine Inglis is well paid; she won't eavesdrop. There are two other prostitutes in the house; nobody thinks it odd when people drift in and out of the building." He reached inside his breast pocket and handed a scrap of rice paper to Garnett. "Take a look at this," he said, "and tell me what you make of it."

He found himself looking at a sketch map of what appeared to be a restricted area, the perimeter of which consisted of a high concrete wall with a watch tower set in each corner. Inside the compound were five single-storey buildings, four of which formed a square around the fifth hut which bore a red cross. The symbols on the sketch map indicated that anti-personnel mines had been laid inside the wall; the scale told him that the average minefield depth was twenty-five metres. Just inside the main entrance was another oblong shaped building marked Guardroom, opposite which, jutting out from the east wall, was an office labelled Governor.

Garnett looked up and said, "This is a plan of the new detention centre at Parkhurst."

"Correct, what else do you know about the area?"

"Not much. The centre was built on the site of Albany Barracks, next door to the prison on the road leading to Cowes. There is a hospital almost opposite which the Russians used as a barracks for the security battalion guarding the Centre. That's about all I know; they were still building the place when I escaped."

Vickers said, "The hospital is still used as a barracks, and a

121

number of helicopter pads have been built in the grounds. We know they have three HOUNDS on permanent alert. One of the three helicopters is a gun ship, the other two are earmarked for troop lift. As for the watch towers, each is occupied by two men with a 7.62mm. PKS general purpose machine gun; there is a sentry on the main gate and eight more prowling the compound with guard dogs. At any one time, the number of men resting in the guardroom will number two officers and thirty-six soldiers. And if that isn't enough, there are four armed warders in the reception centre which is directly underneath the governor's office. The Russians are responsible for security, the British provide the governor and prison staff. It could be a tough nut to crack open."

"You're not thinking of trying, are you?"

Vickers stubbed out his cigarette and lit another. He walked over to the window, drew the curtain to one side and looked down into the square. "That hut in the centre," he said slowly, "the one marked with the red cross, that's the prison hospital. Pollard is in there."

Garnett said; "That's impossible, Endicott told me he was dead."

"Then Endicott was mistaken. Pollard was brought out of the flat alive but in very bad shape. An officer from Special Branch recognised him and he was therefore flown to Parkhurst. I suspect that in fact someone tipped Special Branch off but that is beside the point. I understand the surgeons removed a bullet from his groin, left shoulder and left lung, and my informant tells me he will be fit for questioning within the next two to three days. Pollard was a member of the Central Committee, he knows the top men in the Resistance. We simply can't allow him to be interrogated."

"I think you had better run for cover while there is still time."

Vickers allowed the curtain to fall back into place and turned to face Garnett again. "I'm afraid that won't do."

Garnett said, "I don't know what you have in mind, General, but I want no part of it."

"Pollard need only name the other four in his cell to implicate thousands, literally thousands. Do you believe that?"

"Frankly, no."

122

Vickers perched himself on the windowsill, crossing one slim leg over the other. "He was one of the pioneers, Garnett, responsible for rural and urban operations north of the Thames, East Anglia, and as far west as Oxford. He broke his area up into ten districts and appointed a commander for each one. These commanders in turn found five group leaders and each group leader found five cell leaders and each cell leader selected five section leaders, and at every level in this chain there were cut outs and message centres to provide security for the one hundred and twenty-five active units in each district."

He paused for effect and then said slowly; "Pollard's area of responsibility therefore embraced a total of 1250 units and there were four others in his cell, each of whom controlled a similar number. So you see the Special Branch has a unique opportunity to break in at the top and crumble the organisation downwards at least as far as the first cut out."

"And where does that occur?"

"At the Group Message Centre."

Garnett said; "General, suppose Pollard does name the other four and they all talk; by my reckoning, in the worst case, we can lose about 250 before the first cut outs become effective. That's a long way short of thousands."

Vickers stretched out an arm and ejected the smouldering butt from his cigarette holder into a brass ashtray. "Isn't that rather a fine debating point?" he said.

"Perhaps. I'll give you another. What right had Pollard, in his position, to go glory hunting? If he is as important as you make out, he should have steered clear of trouble."

"You aren't related to Pollard, by any chance? You have the same name and your outlook is similar in many ways." He waited for a reply, and not getting one, went on, "There was of course more than one Seymour in the old peacetime army which explains why Special Branch managed to get the photograph of the wrong man on the Wanted List."

"I happen to have two sisters but no brother. Does that set your mind at rest?"

123

"It's not really a question of my mind being at rest. I'd like to know how you are going to feel when, to quote your own figure, we lose those 250 men. I chose you because I thought you were the best man for the job. You know the area and you've been inside the prison. I can of course find someone else, but he will have less time in which to plan the job and probably less chance of success."

Garnett said, "I don't know why I should feel guilty about turning you down, particularly in view of what has happened in the last day or two."

"I hope you don't think I had anything to do with that. Coleman is not like you and I; he has a rather narrow view of what loyalty entails. I'd like you to know that his orders were countermanded as soon as we heard the details." Vickers cocked his head on one side. "Well?" he said.

"Well what?"

"Are you going to do it or not?"

He had been offered a choice but in reality there was no choice. A lifetime's habit isn't cast aside overnight, old codes of behaviour die hard. To walk away from this situation would be a betrayal of all he stood for. On a lower moral plane, he had a feeling that he couldn't last much longer because in the last few days his luck seemed to be running out. In the back of his mind was the idea that if he did this one last job he might be able to drive a bargain with Vickers.

"What do you want me to do about Pollard?" he said quietly.

Relief showed in Vickers' face. "Well now," he said heavily, "that's a good question. There are two schools of thought on the subject of Pollard. One maintains that he must be silenced at all costs. Not only do I regard that as unethical, it's also impractical. We have just one informant inside Parkhurst and I can assure you no amount of money would persuade him to risk his neck in any violent enterprise; and that leaves us with only one option."

Garnett shifted his position in the chair and crossed his legs. "We shall have to spring him," he said.

"Correct. My operation branch produced a plan to storm the prison."

"With what?"

Vickers rubbed his eyes. "The local Resistance group could put about thirty men into the field. They have a couple of general purpose machine guns, one Wombat anti-tank gun and an 81mm. mortar."

"It's a non starter, we're up against five hundred combat troops."

"Oh, I agree with you. We've come up with something a little more subtle, on the Trojan Horse principle. I propose to stage the arrest of someone who is on their wanted list and deliver that person to the prison."

"And they would be expecting us?"

"Of course."

"And we could make it stand up?"

"I can guarantee the cover plan will be perfect," said Vickers.

"All right. We can get as far as Reception, then what?"

"Then you have to start fighting."

Garnett picked up the scrap of rice paper and studied it closely. An idea was beginning to take shape in his mind.

Vickers said, "Of course the other snag is getting Pollard out. It won't be easy, he's a stretcher case."

"We'll go through the wall."

"What about the minefield?"

"We'll go through that too. I take it I'll get some help."

"Of course, I'm here to see you get every assistance."

"That's nice," said Garnett, "how long have I got?"

"A maximum of two to three days from now, by which time we calculate they will have him on LSD."

"And I can count on getting four or five men into the prison with me."

"About one car load," said Vickers.

"So," said Garnett, "I take four in with me." He held up his fingers and began to enumerate the items. "I must have Cortex, safety fuse, primers, detonators, plastic explosive and polythene tubing. I also need two or three shoulder controlled missiles. Either Miniman or the Russian RPG 7 will do. The car must be rigged with a quick release for the luggage compartment which can be triggered

125

from inside the car. I am going to have someone concealed inside the boot, so the car has to be something the size of a Zephyr. Can you manage all that?"

"I think so."

Garnett said; "It isn't a question of thinking, if you can't provide the kit it's no go. I want a top notch marksman and a demolition expert, I want two Jaguars which are identical right down to the registration plates, and I shall want the local Resistance to provide a diversion outside the prison. I need someone for the get away car, and he has to be good, and I mean really good. Finally I want Markham and Halliday on the team."

"May I ask why?" said Vickers.

"Because I know them and because I need at least two men who look like, act like, think like, and even smell like policemen. I shall want to meet the head of the local Resistance as soon as possible and I must also talk to your informer."

"All right, Garnett, we shall do our best."

"Good," said Garnett, "I'll leave the arrangements in your hands, but remember this, it's important that I get the marksman into the governor's office where he can cover the yard. I suggest we nominate him as the wanted man."

"There will be no difficulty about that."

"I shall want to run my eye over the people you select, General." Garnett smiled briefly. "Just to make sure they meet with my approval—if they don't they are out. Is that understood?"

Vickers stood up and glanced at his watch. "I must be going," he said.

"There is just one thing more," said Garnett. "If we pull this off we are going to be hot. I'd like you to make arrangements to get us all out of the country including a girl called Valerie Dane."

Vickers raised an eyebrow. "That might prove difficult," he said, "but not entirely impossible." He walked towards the door and stood facing it, apparently mesmerised by something in the panelling. "It's a spy hole," he said by way of explanation, "I suggest you use it before you go into the other room. Could be embarrassing otherwise. You'll spend the night here. Tomorrow at

126

nine-thirty I want you on the northbound platform at Knights-bridge. Endicott will meet you there."

"Endicott?"

"Certainly. Don't worry, he will be very co-operative. His head is also on the chopping block."

"You will have to do something about my charwoman. My continued absence might strike her as being peculiar."

"My dear Garnett," Vickers said loftily, "we have already taken care of her."

"You think of everything don't you?" Garnett said bitterly. He held up the map. "What do you want done with this?" he asked.

"Eat it," said Vickers, "it won't harm you."

14

The poster had been defaced. Someone had blacked out the front teeth and added a moustache to the upper lip. The dauber had pencilled in the pubic hair on the girl's bikini and a crude phallic symbol dangled from the beach ball which she held in her hands. The poster said 'Beautiful Brighton.'

He stood facing the billboard watching Endicott out of the corner of his eye. An elderly woman, trailing a black French poodle, meandered up and down the platform, a porter emptied the litter bins without enthusiasm. Endicott gave no sign of having seen him.

Garnett went back to his newspaper again and reread the short paragraph on the back page. It did not tell him when Lethbridge's body had been found and the concluding statement that enquiries were proceeding was scarcely informative.

The distant signal changed from red to green and a faint current of air brushed against his legs. He glanced in Endicott's direction again and saw him imperceptibly nod his head as the Uxbridge train roared out of the tunnel and drew up alongside the platform. He followed Endicott into the carriage and sat facing him across the aisle. Endicott retreated behind a newspaper.

Nothing happened until they got to Barons Court when Robinson got into the same compartment and stood in the doorway. He was still dressed as a railwayman and carried a respirator haversack slung over one shoulder. Endicott didn't appear to notice him. The compartment emptied at Hammersmith but Endicott waited until they were passing through Ravenscourt Park before he made his move. He got up, looked pointedly at Garnett and walked towards Robinson. Garnett followed him.

Endicott said; "This is your demolition expert."

128

"No."

"What do you mean, NO?" said Endicott.

"He's coloured."

"Now look, man," said Robinson, moving towards Garnett and balling up his fists, "I don't have to take that kind of talk from you."

Garnett put a restraining hand on his shoulder. "In London," he said patiently, "you can pass in a crowd because people here are used to seeing West Indians every day of their lives; in the Isle of Wight it would be different, you would stand out."

"We can get him on to the Island," said Endicott, "and nobody will think twice about him, I guarantee it."

"You'd better be right." Garnett pulled on the lobe of his ear. "You're a demolition expert are you?"

"I did four years with the 75th Assault Engineer Regiment."

"I can handle a rifle but I couldn't get into the first hundred at Bisley to save my life."

"I was a sergeant," said Robinson, "I've handled every type of explosive you can name, and I can do anything you want with me eyes closed."

Garnett smiled. "I want a path blown through a minefield and you'd better have your eyes open when you do it. I might also need a hole in a wall."

"I'll need P.E., cortex..."

Garnett cut him off. "I know what you want," he said. "Can you handle a Miniman or RPG 7?"

"Some."

"I want you to hit a building."

"For a moment," said Robinson, "I thought you had a pinpoint target in mind."

"This is a pinpoint target, you are going to put three shots in through a window."

Robinson shrugged his shoulders. "So, I'll have to be good," he said.

"You will. Are you married?"

"I've got four kids to prove it."

"I should tell you that our prospects are not good."

"What's that supposed to mean?"

"It means this is your chance to back out."

"What happens to my family if I snuff it?"

"They will be taken care of," said Endicott.

"Well I'll tell you," said Robinson, "for all their propaganda, these Russians don't like us any better than do most of you folk. Are we going to kill us some Ivans?"

"We are," said Garnett.

"Well then, man, that's okay by me," Robinson said flatly.

Endicott said; "We are going to get off the train at Acton. Robinson will go on to Ealing. A contact will call on him later this afternoon to give him further instructions."

"I need to brief him," said Garnett.

Endicott was both calm and indifferent. He eyed Garnett up and down. "You can brief him after he arrives on the Island. I'll tell you where and when."

He turned away and moved down to the far end of the compartment. So far as Endicott was concerned, the interview was over. Garnett nodded goodbye to Robinson and joined him by the door. They got out at Acton, crossed over the bridge and caught a train back to Hammersmith.

The Billiard Hall was above Wainwright's bakery and a Jewish delicatessen which was no longer in business. A wooden staircase led up to the hall, an oblong shaped room containing three full sized tables, a beer bar, and a heavy concentration of stale tobacco smoke which made the eyes water and the stomach heave. Except for the lights above the end table nearest the bar, the hall was in darkness. As his eyes became accustomed to the gloom, Garnett could see the vague silhouette of a man standing in the shadows behind the pool of light above the table. Endicott snapped his fingers, and the man, billiard cue in hand, moved up to the table and into the light.

Endicott said; "Charlie Baker, you met him four days ago. Tell us about yourself, Charlie."

"What do you want to know?"

"It's not like you to be modest, Charlie. Don't be coy, you're

130

among friends."

"I'm a driver," said Baker, "the best you'll find in the Smoke. I've pulled jobs with the South London Gang, and Tony Weaver and Dandy Hughie Spinks when they were in business before the war. Everybody who had class wanted me."

Baker sighted the cue and sent the white ball rolling up the table to make the break. "I've got a photographic memory, you see. Show me a street plan or a map and I've got the route taped. I don't have to make a dry run, see. Makes for security, that's why I was always in demand."

He sent a red ball into the bottom right hand pocket and left the cue ball in a position to pot the blue into the centre pocket. He sank another red, took the black and tried a fancy off-cushion shot for the next red which failed to come off. "You have a job in mind?" he asked.

"A big and risky one," said Garnett.

"How much do I get paid?"

"Five thousand," said Endicott.

"Pounds or dollars?"

"Whichever you prefer."

"Dollars plus transportation to a neutral country."

Garnett turned to Endicott. "Is this man in the Resistance or not?" he said incredulously.

"You think I should do it for nothing," said Baker. "What do you think I am going to live on? Fresh air? Don't tell me you are doing this job for nothing. Your friend has agreed to my fee, so either put up or fucking shut up."

Baker smashed a red ball into the top pocket.

"We'll find someone else," said Garnett.

"We won't," Endicott said firmly, "he's the best there is. Do you think we can produce a Graham Hill or a Bruce Maclaren at the drop of a hat? Baker is all right; he won't let you down, I guarantee it."

Garnett flushed angrily. "By God," he said, "you're giving out a lot of guarantees this norning with little or no prospect of having to pick up the liability."

Baker lit a cigarette. "How difficult is this job?" he said.

131

"Our chances are about five to one against. I imagine those odds don't appeal to you."

"I don't see you laughing."

"Thinking of backing out?" Garnett asked.

Baker sank the pink, walked round the table, took the pink out of the bottom pocket and put it back on the spot.

"I'm raising my price to seventy-five hundred," he said. Endicott opened his mouth to protest but didn't get the chance because Baker cut the ground under his feet. "Payable after the job is finished, okay?"

"It's a deal," said Endicott.

"Good. When do we start?"

"This afternoon, you'll be told what to do."

"You know where to find me," said Baker.

"We certainly do," Endicott said with feeling.

"Be seeing you then." Baker leaned over the table and lined up a red. Just as they reached the door, he said, "By the way, what sort of car am I driving?"

"A Jaguar," said Garnett.

Baker grunted. "Too common," he said. "Bogies are always on the look out for Jags. You should have picked a family saloon."

"It has to be a Jaguar," said Garnett. They walked out into the bright sunlight.

It was hotter than most days in midsummer and heat waves danced and shimmered above the sticky asphalt, and men shed jackets and walked about in shirt sleeves and braces, and women changed into silk dresses and small boys paddled in play pools. It was definitely not the sort of day on which to pound the pavements with a wet shirt sticking to your back.

They walked the length of the Broadway, hopped a bus as far as Gloucester Road where they took to the tube once more, switching trains time and time again. It seemed to Garnett that they doubled back and forth across their tracks more times than it was strictly necessary to do.

Towards noon they left the train at South Harrow and made their way to Lemon and Meakin, a small firm which turned out precision tools in a factory built under the arches of the viaduct. At first sight, the arches appeared to be completely bricked up until the eye caught sight of the ventilation and air conditioning intake in the cornice, and the narrow steel door which afforded entrance into the works. Set into the wall, on the left side of the door, was a button marked service. Endicott pressed it hopefully.

A little, stooped old man opened the door. His watery eyes blinked behind steel framed glasses and he nervously brushed the straggling, nicotine stained moustache which adorned his upper lip. He opened his mouth but the noise level was such that they couldn't hear what he said. Endicott bent down and shouted into his ear, and although Garnett didn't hear anything, the old man appeared to understand.

He led them through the shop, nimbly avoiding the unguarded driving belts which snaked across the floor. Not one of the lathe operators or machinists looked up as they went by.

The works office was at the far end of the shop. It had the advantage of being sound proof, and after the bedlam outside, it seemed as quiet as a monastery. The works manager was in his early thirties and had a perpetual worried look on his face which went with his balding head. According to the name plate on the desk, his name was Grimes.

He rose to his feet as they entered, waited until the old man had left them, and then said; "You're three minutes late." His voice was hoarse and urgent. "In another two minutes you would have missed the train and the next one isn't due until twelve thirty-five."

Endicott was unruffled. "Are we all set?" he said.

Grimes moved round the desk, brushed past Endicott and locked the office door. He walked back again, reached under the desk and tripped a switch. A panel in the side wall of the office slid back smoothly. He then killed the overhead fluorescent lighting.

Garnett found himself staring into a black void. A split second later lights appeared outside the office and he saw that he was looking into a sort of tunnel, which extended well beyond either side of the office and ran parallel to it. The lights were to his left and illuminated a sand bagged wall mounted on a trolley.

133

Grimes said; "The tunnel is one hundred metres long and pretty well sound proof, but to make sure we will wait for the train. I'm going to give you a small box on which there are ten buttons. Each button will operate two metal targets each measuring forty by forty millimetres. The targets fall when hit. You can press the buttons in any order you like. The marksman has a 7.62mm. FN self loading rifle with telescopic sights. The representative range is four hundred metres, and the test is to get twenty hits in fifteen seconds."

Grimes pressed the box into his hand. "Don't start until I give the word," he said. "I'm going to signal the marksman to stand by."

In the stillness of the room, Garnett could distinctly hear both men breathing quickly. It seemed an eternity before Grimes finished checking the luminous face of his wrist watch and said, "Okay, anytime you like."

He began to press the buttons in haphazard order, counting off the seconds aloud. It was like watching a silent movie. The small white plates appeared at varying heights and angles and fell amost instantly. If he had not been able to see the strike of shot in the sandbagged wall, Garnett would have said it was a put up job. By the time he had counted to fourteen, all twenty targets were down. It was an exhibition of accurate and sustained rapid shooting the like of which he had not seen before.

Grimes switched the fluorescent lights on again. He bent over the desk, selected a button on the intercom and said; "All right, that's it. Pick up the empty shells and come into the office. Use the door at the bottom of the range."

Endicott said; "What do you think?"

Garnett cleared his throat. "It's almost unbelievable, I've never seen anything like it."

"You're happy about this marksman, are you?"

"I couldn't want for anyone better."

"Good," said Endicott, "don't go and change your mind."

The door behind the desk opened inwards, and Dane stepped into the room carrying the FN slung over her shoulder and a hatful of empty cases in her hands. She was wearing fawn coloured slacks and a black nylon roll neck sweater with long sleeves.

134

"Your marksman," Endicott said smugly. His voice almost purred.

Garnett balled up his fists. For a moment he wanted to drive them into Endicott's face and then just as quickly as he had flared up, he calmed down. "Find someone else," he said wearily.

"No," said Dane.

Her jaw was set and determined. A muscle twitched near her left eye. She dropped the hatful of shells on to the desk and then carefully placed the FN alongside them. She caressed the stock of the rifle almost lovingly. She looked up and smiled wanly at Garnett. "You can't get rid of me as easily as that, and besides where would you find anyone who is even half as good as what I am?"

Garnett turned to Endicott and said; "Perhaps you and Grimes could leave us alone for five minutes."

"So long as it isn't more than five minutes. We haven't got all day."

Garnett waited until they were alone and then said, quite simply, "Why?"

She picked up a pencil and began to doodle on the desk blotter.

"Are you tired of life or didn't they tell you what is involved?"

"They said it will be a very hazardous operation."

"Then why risk your neck, for heaven's sake?"

"Because I knew you had been talked into doing it," she said.

She flushed and looked down at the blotter again, and pressed so hard on the pencil that it went through the blotter and broke off at the point.

"I don't want anything to happen to you," Garnett said quietly, "that's why I am going to ask you to drop out." He leaned forward on the desk. "If we do pull it off, they are going to hunt us down, and they will not rest until they have accounted for every single one of us, and I don't want to see you running scared."

"Listen," she said softly, "don't let's argue about it any more. Where you go, I go, it's as simple as that."

The pencil snapped in two.

"Look," said Garnett, "don't you realise that you are already assured of a ticket to get out of this country, you don't have to earn

135

it the hard way."

She reared back and he knew he could not have hurt her more if
he had slapped her face, and hurting Dane was the last thing he
wanted.

"You need a sniper," she said coldly, "I am the best there is. With
me you stand a chance, without me, you stand no chance
whatsoever."

Endicott opened the door and came into the office. "I'm sorry,"
he said rudely, "but time is running on and we have a lot to do." He
glanced at Dane and smiled thinly. "Garnett hasn't talked you out of
it has he?"

She shook her head. "Nobody can talk me out of anything once I
have made up my mind."

"Good," said Endicott. "From the moment you walk out of here
you are Janet Prentice, alias Jane Carlisle, alias Susan Miles. I don't
have to remind you that the Secret Service have been looking for her
for the past two and a half years. They are going to catch up with
her in Sandown the day after tomorrow in Woolworth's at
ten-twenty in the morning."

As Endicott droned on, it seemed to Garnett that Dane had
already lost her identity and the chances were that in less than
forty-eight hours she would be dead. He remembered seeing the
wanted list displayed in the Cavendish Hotel, when he was up in
York, and recalled that Janet Prentice, the number two on the list
who had died eighteen months ago, had been a dark woman with
short black hair. They were putting up a tempting enough bait all
right because it wasn't every day of the week that Special Branch
had the chance to lay their hands on the head of Intelligence for
South-East England; but there was just one snag—Dane and Prentice
were about as much alike as chalk and cheese.

"Grimes will give you all the dope," said Endicott. He jerked his
head in the direction of the door. "You'd better cut along now," he
said.

Dane glanced at Garnett, a lopsided smile on her face, and then
walked out without saying a word. The smile was enough; it said
goodbye.

Endicott said, "We'll take a walk, tie up a few details and then you can catch your train." He primed his Dunhill pipe and lit it. "How many do you think they have on their side?" he asked casually.

"Between five and six hundred, why?"

"I just wondered. Six hundred professionals, and what have we got? One villain, two Jacks, one Spade, a Dolly, and a Mouth Piece."

He had had just about enough of Endicott to last him a lifetime. The smug, heavy, self satisfied face smirking at him behind a cloud of foul smelling tobacco smoke got under his skin.

Garnett walked closer. "I'll tell you one thing, Endicott," he said, "whether we succeed or not, they will know they have been hit."

His fist travelled six inches and caught Endicott in the belly. "I'm terribly sorry," said Garnett, "I meant to pull my punch."

He almost sounded sincere.

15

Garnett sat by the open window and swept the glasses across the bay from Culver Cliff to the landslip at Bonchurch, and then back again to the pier, finally training them on the man who was sitting in the lee of a shelter near the theatre.

He was fishing, at least Garnett supposed he was, since there was a rod by his side but he could, just as easily, have been asleep. It was hard to tell because the hat was pulled down over his eyes to shield them against the setting sun. Two other men were fishing off the pier but they were some distance away from the man in whom Garnett was interested.

An elderly couple, who had been admiring the view from a bench seat on the front, got up and went down on to the beach. A longshoreman was repairing a stack of deck chairs outside his store hut, and a stray dog meandered along the promenade, pausing at each lamp post to leave a visiting card. Garnett put the binoculars away and left the room.

The tide was on the turn but it was hardly noticeable because the sea was as calm as a millpond. Garnett sauntered along the promenade and walked up the short flight of steps on to the pier. A few posters, advertising last year's Sunshine Bay Review, still adorned the front of the theatre. A schoolgirl was necking with her boy friend behind one of the slot machines.

The gaps between the planks had a hypnotic effect and he found himself looking down at the sea which was lapping gently against the concrete piles. He jerked his head up, and changing direction, strolled across to where the fisherman was sitting on a canvas stool. Garnett paused at the guard rail and turned his back on the sea.

"Caught anything?" he said.

The fisherman pushed the hat to the back of his head. He had a cherubic face, warm, plump, merry and friendly. He could have been any age between twenty-five and forty.

"They are not biting, too lazy, must be the weather."

"Perhaps you are using the wrong sort of bait," said Garnett.

"Could be; but I've never had much luck with this rod."

"You want to try a Garnett."

"How expensive is it?"

"What have you in mind?"

"Twelve at the most, it's all I can raise."

Garnett said; "I'm told you have a wombat and an 81mm. mortar."

"We-have, but we're short of ammunition, fifteen for the mortar and seven rounds for the wombat."

The schoolgirl with boyfriend in tow appeared round the corner of the theatre and passed within a few feet of them. They were looking into one another's eyes, and they seemed oblivious of everyone else but Garnett didn't believe in taking unnecessary chances.

"It's a beautiful spot," he said.

"Your first visit?"

"Yes, but it won't be my last."

"You should see Blackgang and Alum Bay before you leave. Both are a must for tourists."

The couple disappeared from sight behind the pavilion at the head of the pier.

Garnett said; "I need the wombat to take out the towers on the east side and then punch a hole through the wall. If possible, I have to prevent the Russians reinforcing the prison, so we'll put the 81mm. mortar on to the barracks and thicken up the fire with a couple of general purpose machine guns which can also cover our withdrawal through Newport. Can you manage that?"

"It won't be easy because Newport is a restricted area, and every now and then they have a habit of searching vehicles coming into the town. We could break the machine guns down into small packages and lessen the chance of them being discovered, but the wombat," he

139

shook his head, "Well that's going to be quite a problem. When do I have to be ready?"

"Eleven o'clock the day after tomorrow."

"I'll try but I don't promise anything."

Garnett offered the fisherman a cigarette and lit one himself. "Just do your best," he said, "no one can ask for more than that. Where are you going to put the mortar?"

The fisherman looked up and shielded his eyes against the sun. "I don't think it need really concern you," he said.

"It's a question of timing," said Garnett. "I don't want the bombs to arrive too soon. I imagine the mortar will be somewhere within a five thousand metre radius of the prison. I have three mitre transistorised radio sets no bigger than the palm of your hand, but Newport is surrounded by hills which could effectively screen the radio transmissions. It might be as well if you could contact the mortar position by telephone, just in case the mitre doesn't work."

"When do you want us to start firing?"

"Three minutes after my car has entered the prison gates."

The fisherman stood up and flipped his cigarette into the sea. "What sort of car do you have?" he said quietly.

"I'll let you know when I see you tomorrow," said Garnett. "Not much point in you knowing that unless you can deliver the goods, is there?"

"All right," said the fisherman, "St. Luke's Church, six o'clock, we can talk before choir practice."

"Good. I shall want to brief the switch drivers at the same time. All three of them. Just make sure they are in the choir."

"I told you, I can only raise a dozen."

"Well, you work it out," said Garnett, "four on the machine guns, one look out, two for the mortar and two on the wombat still leaves you with three to play with by my reckoning." He dropped his cigarette on to the broadwalk and crushed it under his heel. "See you in church," he said.

The bus dropped Garnett at the top of the slipway. He knew that the informer would be waiting for him in Stainforth's boat yard, and yet, for some reason which he couldn't explain, he was in no hurry to meet him.

A faint breeze was coming off the millpond sea, and across the water, the lights of Southampton lit the cloud base with an orange glare. It wasn't the most enthralling vista he'd ever seen but it held his attention. It occurred to him that this had once been the busiest stretch of seaway in the world until a reorientation of trade from West to East had largely diminished the status of Southampton as an ocean terminal. He wondered if the old days would ever return in his lifetime.

He sauntered down to the water's edge and walked along the slipway until he came to Stainforth's boat yard. As boat yards went it was singularly small and unimpressive. Pre-war it might have provided work for twenty or so men, but now it was virtually derelict. Immediately after the war it had been taken over as a co-operative and then turned into a sort of exclusive do-it-yourself club. It was exclusive because membership was restricted to the staff of Parkhurst Prison.

He pushed open the gate and went inside. A light was burning in one of the sheds where a man in dungarees was rubbing down the hull of a dinghy. Garnett skirted a pool of murky water and crunched across the gravel towards the shed. The man in the dungarees watched him all the way.

"I'm Sam Coleridge," Garnett said quietly, "I'm looking for a mariner called Taylor."

The man said; "I'm he, but I am not so ancient." He wiped his hands on a piece of waste. "What can I do for you?"

"I want to know about the man in the prison hospital, the one who was brought in about a week ago."

Taylor leaned back against the boat. "Oh, him," he said, "I can't tell you much because no Brit is allowed near him. They brought that one in by chopper, and the Russians have had him under wraps ever since. Got an armed guard at his bedside night and day, so I hear. I believe he is now sitting up and taking notice, so his operation must have been a success."

"All right," said Garnett, "tell me something about Reception.

141

What's the procedure when a prisoner is admitted?"

"He is mugged, fingerprinted, stripped, searched, and then medically examined. Reception is just inside the prison gates on the left and is underneath the Governor's office. There are five warders and two Russians on duty in the block."

Garnett looked up sharply. "I understood there were only four warders," he said.

"Then you were misinformed, unless your man overlooked the assistant governor and his escort."

"The assistant governor?" Garnett queried.

"Major General Vishinsky, MGB. He's just been appointed. We hear he is going to take over from Laker. Seems the Russians believe we're too sympathetic towards the prisoners, although if you clapped eyes on the two wardresses in Reception, you wouldn't think we were soft. A right couple of queers they are. They really enjoy their work."

"Let's get this straight." said Garnett. "There are three British Warders, two Russian escorts and a couple of women jailors?"

"Correct."

"And on each tower," Garnett continued, "there are two sentries and eight prowlers in the compound."

"Right. But don't forget the dogs, four Alsatians, you want to look out for them."

Garnett lit a cigarette. "It seems I am not so badly informed as I thought," he said. "Now tell me what it is like inside Reception."

Taylor rummaged through his pockets and came up with a battered pipe. He filled it carefully and then struck a match on the wall. "You come in through the door." he said between puffs, "and there's a Russian sentry immediately on your left. Facing you is a counter staffed by two warders, behind which is a glass partitioned office where the rest of the Brits hang out. There is a staircase on the left behind the counter which leads up to the Governor's office. Vishinsky shares it with our bloke, and his bodyguard sits facing the door with a sub machine gun across his lap."

A faint bleeping sound caught Garnett's attention, and he motioned Taylor to be silent. It sounded as though the police car

142

was coming straight for them and he broke out into a clammy sweat. Taylor's face was the colour of putty. The car drew closer and then, just as Taylor was beginning to look as if he might make a run for it, the bleeping sound began to fade away.

Taylor sighed audibly and said, "My stomach almost turned over."

"You weren't alone. Perhaps we had better wrap this up and go our separate ways."

"I'm all for that," said Taylor.

"One final thing. Who looks after the prisoners in the cell blocks?"

"The Brit warders. We are responsible for exercising them in the yard but we seem to spend most of our time in the block watching the prisoners sewing mail bags."

"Could you release the prisoners in your block if you wanted to? I mean is it physically possible for you to do so?"

"I could, but I'm not tired of living yet."

"Do the other warders feel the same way?"

Taylor knocked out the pipe on the heel of his shoe. "As far as I know," he said, "I'm the only friend you've got inside the place. If you want my opinion, at best, they will stay inside their cell blocks and do nothing to help you; at worst, they'll don respirators and switch on happy land."

"Happy land?" said Garnett.

"BZ, a very effective mental incapacitating agent which can be dispensed through the ventilating system in each cell block. After five minutes you have a very ga ga set of people on your hands. It has no lasting effects and is rather a neat way of controlling the inmates."

"How about the hospital?"

"Never been inside it," said Taylor, "for all I know they may use something more drastic like Tanus; they've given up shooting people now, you know—a spot of nerve gas does the trick inside a minute."

Garnett checked his wrist watch and saw that he could just make the next bus back if he hurried. "Do you want to go first?" he said.

"Can't. I have to lock up."

143

"Of course," said Garnett. "Thanks for all your help."

He walked out of the yard and caught the bus at the top of the slipway. All the way back to Sandown he thought about BZ and Tabun Agents but all the thinking in the world didn't alter the fact that he had completely overlooked the possibility that the opposition might use chemical weapons.

There was a nagging suspicion in the back of his mind that he had been had. Perhaps Vickers was banking on an each way bet; either they succeeded in getting Pollard out or the Russians gassed him to prevent them doing just that. It was getting to be a case of heads I win, tails you lose.

16

Garnett wiped away the sweat which had gathered on his forehead and was beginning to run into his eyes. The unseasonable heatwave showed no signs of abating and he wondered how much longer the weather would continue to hold good. Across the road from where he was standing, there was a ramshackle building with a corrugated iron roof on which was mounted a signboard which said, Wates' Garage, Rebuilds are our speciality. He walked across the road and went inside.

The floor was littered with grease cans, oil slick, and open tool boxes. A pair of feet stuck out from underneath an ancient Ford Prefect. A greasy hand, clutching an adjustable spanner, appeared briefly and tapped the brake drum for no apparent good reason except that it made a dull clanging noise.

"Where is Townsend?" said Garnett.

"Out back, working on the Jag," said a muffled voice.

"Mind if I go through and have a word with him?"

"Help yourself."

"Thanks," said Garnett.

The Jaguar was tucked away in a lean-to which overlooked an open field. Baker was under the bonnet tinkering with the 3.5 litre engine, tuning it up to a fine pitch, and the noise level was such that he didn't hear Garnett approach and only reacted when Garnett reached inside the car and turned the ignition off.

"For fuck sake knock it off," he shouted. He emerged from under the bonnet and then said, "Oh, it's you." He slammed the bonnet down.

Baker wiped his hands on his overalls, felt for the cigarette butt lodged behind his ear and stuck it in his mouth. Garnett gave him a light.

"Did you have any trouble on the way over?" he said.

"No bother at all. There really is someone by the name of Townsend; I had his re-entry permit."

"What about the car?"

Baker patted the wing affectionately. "I can guarantee she'll go like a bird. A ton and a half with no sweat. I've even managed to get her tanked up with 5 star; none of your old utility grade for this baby."

"That's fine," said Garnett. He reached inside his breast pocket and brought out a road map which he unfolded on the bonnet of the car. "You are supposed to have a photographic memory," he said, "so you had better put it to work. This is a street plan of Newport; there's the prison and here is the street where you will be waiting. I want you there at eleven-fifteen tomorrow on the dot. Not a minute before or a minute after. You stall the car and tinker with the engine while you wait for the signal. When you see two green flares go up, you come like the wind down the road, turn right at the corner and mid way between the two watch towers on the east wall you'll see a hole in the wall. That is where you pick us up."

"How many are there of you?" said Baker.

"I don't know."

"What do you mean you don't know? How many are you taking in with you?"

"Four."

"And you're bringing someone out. That makes six of us in all. Hell, you'll never get that number into the Jag."

"I never thought I would. Most of us won't make it back."

Baker took the butt out of his mouth and flipped it outside on to the grass. He smiled crookedly; "I'm beginning to think I quoted too low a price for the job," he said.

"People have been known to go bankrupt like that," said Garnett. He rubbed his chin and pointed to the map again. "Watch the hill leading down into Newport, it's steep and we have to make a sharp left turn into a one way street where a Jaguar, identical to ours, will be parked. As soon as we pass, it will pull out and follow us through

146

the town. We take the road over the Downs to Brading while the decoy heads for Ryde."

Garnett took out a pencil and drew a rough sketch map on the back of an envelope. "About four miles out of Newport, you come to an S-bend and the road skirts a gorse covered heath. You will see a track on your right which leads into the bushes where a Dormobile will be waiting. That's where you drop us off. The track circles back to the road. About two miles from Brading there is a lane on the left hand side of the road. Go down it and turn into the first farm you come to. There will be a horse box in the yard into which you will drive the Jaguar. Close the doors of the horse box, make your way through the farmyard and head for the copse at the bottom of the hill. You will find a woodcutter's shed in the copse, where a bicycle will be hidden. Take it, and ride back to this place and await further instructions. Is that clear?"

"One question. What happens if I don't see any green flares?"

"You go home," said Garnett, "and you don't collect the seventy-five hundred." He smiled briefly, "You can keep the map and envelope," he said.

There are a good many ways of killing time pleasantly. Lying on a bed and staring up at the ceiling while the mind entertains dark thoughts is not one of them. His palms were slippery with sweat and the weather had nothing to do with it. Garnett closed his eyes and he could see the man twitching like an animated puppet. His eyes and nose were streaming, and he was both defecating and urinating because he could no longer control his bowels. In one minute he would be dead because nerve gas acted as quickly as that, but what happened to the mind in that one minute? Did it disintegrate with the rest of the nervous system or were you aware of what was happening to you? Garnett thought there was a distinct possibility that he might know the answer to that question tomorrow.

In an effort to take his mind off the subject, he picked up the newspaper, which was lying on the floor, and scanned the headlines again. It was not an altogether fortunate choice.

The Identi-kit picture was on the front page, and it was still a

147

relief to see that the man bore no resemblance to himself. They had given him a narrow pointed face prominent ears and bushy eyebrows, but the girl was uncannily like Dane. The high cheek-bones, the eyes, the angle of her jaw and the hair styling were exactly right, even to the point where the artist had sketched in the upward curve of the lips at the corners of her mouth which gave the impression that something amused her. It seemed that the ticket collector had remembered more than just the shape of her legs. He blacked out the hair with a ballpoint pen to see what difference it made, but even with short dark hair, the picture, to his jaundiced eye, looked remarkably like Dane. He threw the paper to one side in disgust.

Perhaps his imagination was running wild. Perhaps after all they would get away with it, and Vickers would keep his word and they would start a new life together in a new land. But getting out of England was no easy matter.

There were two ways out of the country: you either went via Eire or Spain, and neither route was exactly a picnic. Eire was for the VIPs and the least hazardous once you got across the Irish Sea, since you merely had to sit it out in your safe haven until a submarine was available to pick you up off the beach. He considered it unlikely that they would rate VIP treatment, which left them with the Spanish route.

He had no first hand knowledge of anyone who had travelled the Spanish route successfully, and it was hardly surprising when you considered what was involved. It was a long, slow, dangerous process from the moment you arrived in Brixham, waited for the right weather conditions and then made it across the channel to a landfall in Brittany, when you were then in the hands of the French Underground who undertook to see you safely over the Pyrenees.

Garnett got up from the bed and stood by the window. A girl with long blonde hair was exercising her dog on the sands below. From the back, she looked just like Dane and he felt a sudden uplift of spirit, until the girl turned round and he saw that the dying sun was merely playing tricks with his eyesight. He reached for his jacket and left the room.

He entered St Luke's by a side door, and although the church was empty, he elected to sit in a pew at the back. The setting sun played on the stained glass window behind the altar and reflected the mosaic on to the stone floor by the pulpit.

The stillness had a relaxing effect on Garnett. He thought it curious that, in the end, everything depended on Dane. If she failed to show up in the morning, they could do nothing, and resultantly at least half a dozen men would still be alive by this time tomorrow night. And yet, if Pollard talked a whole lot more than six men would be dead. It suddenly occurred to him that perhaps Pollard might not want to be rescued; he might prefer to remain inside the prison hospital where at least, for the time being, he knew what the future held in store for him. It was asking a lot to expect a man in his physical shape to go over the wall.

An elderly woman, wearing glasses, came into the church and tiptoed up the centre aisle. She crossed herself before the altar, and then, turning to her left, disappeared behind the choir stalls. Moments later, the organ burst into Bach's Toccata and Fugue; the door to the vestry opened and the fisherman beckoned to Garnett to come inside.

There were three other men waiting for him whose faces he preferred not to remember. The fisherman said; "It is best if we stick to nicknames. This is Tom, Dick and Harry."

Garnett shook hands with each man in turn. "Well," he said jovially, "who fancies himself as a hot rod driver?"

It was the wrong approach. No one spoke up.

Disconcerted, he said, "All right, who has been nicked for speeding?"

"I have," said Harry.

"You'll drive the car then," said Garnett. "A Mr Richardson has hired a Jaguar from Wainwright's Self Drive. Pick it up tomorrow, take it over to Newport, and wait outside Chappells' in the Parade. I want you there at eleven-fifty. About ten minutes later you will see an identical Jaguar pass you. Pull out and follow it as far as the junction of the Ryde and Brading roads. The leading car will go to Brading, you keep on to Ryde. Whatever happens, ditch the car ten

149

minutes after we part company at the junction."

Garnett reached inside his jacket pocket, brought out a manilla envelope and gave it to Harry. "This," he said, "is a driving licence and identity papers to prove that you are Richardson."

Garnett could see doubt beginning to register in every face and he started to speak quickly like a rep trying to win over a sales resistant customer.

Turning to Tom he said: "There's a Dormobile waiting for you at the caravan site down by the railway bridge. I want you to collect it and park it up on St George's Down above Brading tomorrow morning at twelve. There is a track just short of the S-bend on the left of the road as you are going towards Newport. If you go down the track, you can hide the van in amongst the gorse bushes and you will be out of sight of the road. You stay with the van until we arrive. If we don't show up, drive the Dormobile back to the caravan site and leave it."

Garnett paused to clear his throat and then got in again quickly, before anyone had a chance to ask questions.

"Dick will collect a horse box from Copeland's farm in Arreton and deliver it to Copse Heath. In case you don't know, Copse Heath is up for sale. It's a small farm about a mile out of Brading up on the Downs, and is, at present, unoccupied. Put the horse box in the yard and leave the rear doors open and the ramp down so that the Jaguar can drive straight into it. Before you leave the horse box, I want you to look under the driver's seat where you will see something which looks like a pencil, but which has a horizontal split pin near the top. I want you to take the pin out. All right?"

Dick smiled loosely. He was an amiable if not an intelligent man but there were occasions when he was quick on the uptake and this was one of them.

"Sounds like a bomb then," he said. "When do she go off?"

"Somewhere after twelve-fifteen; don't arm it until eleven-fifteen."

Dick said; "I thought this bloke were an overner, Tom. Seems he might be one of us after all."

"And that makes it all right, does it?" said Garnett.

150

"It helps," said Tom.

Garnett produced a couple of key rings and threw one to each man. "The ignition keys," he said briefly. "You'll find the registration number of the vehicle on the tag; you won't need any papers."

"It sounds too easy," Tom said doubtfully.

"I suppose you would be a damn sight happier if the difficulties stuck out a mile?"

"There's no call to be sarcastic, mister. We do have some rights you know, and one of them is being spoken to in a civil manner."

He had a point, and if he had been anyone else, Garnett would have apologised but this man had a whining plaintive voice which got under his skin and without meaning to, he lost his temper.

"After the war is over," said Garnett, "I'll be all sweetness and light, and you can tell me to piss off if you have a mind to, but until it is, I am apt to be quick tempered and nasty to anyone who appears to me to be questioning his orders."

Tom was not impressed. "I still say you have no right to throw your weight around when you're begging favours. You'd look pretty sick if we failed to turn up tomorrow."

Garnett leaned back against a radiator and studied both men carefully. He didn't greatly care for Tom. He had met his type before, he was all mouth and sly talk, a born troublemaker, the sort of factory worker who would have the men out on a wildcat strike before you could say knife.

"If there is a fiasco tomorrow," he said quietly, "you can rest assured there will be an enquiry, and I would not care to be in your shoes if the findings showed you were to blame in part."

The implied threat was there for anyone to see without rubbing their noses in it. The men, embarrassed, looked down at the floor and shuffled their feet.

"Best be getting along then," said Dick.

"See you tomorrow then," said Garnett.

The fisherman said; "I won't be a minute, there are still one or two details I have to sort out." He followed the men out of the room, closing the door behind him.

151

Left alone in the vestry, Garnett cleared a chair of hymn books and sat down, facing a line of off-white surplices hanging from a row of hooks set into the wall. He found a crumpled cigarette left in the packet and tried, unsuccessfully, to smoke it by pinching the slit in the paper between forefinger and thumb. He finally gave it up as a bad job. The fisherman came back ten minutes later wearing a sour expression.

"Having trouble?" said Garnett.

"A little. They were all for packing it in. They think it's too risky."

"Will they turn up tomorrow?"

"Possibly. I wouldn't count on them too much."

"What about the others?"

"They are reliable. Everything is laid on."

"Everything?" Garnett queried.

"Everything; the wombat, the mortar, and the machine guns. I believe we still have a couple of points to clear up."

"We have," said Garnett. "My car is a black Zephyr, registration number VDL 141A, and the mitre radio sets are awaiting collection in the left luggage at Sandown Station." He put his hand in his hip pocket and brought out a slip of paper. "This is the baggage check," he said. "Get somebody to pick them up for you."

The fisherman held out a plump hand. "Well, now," he said, "all that's left is for me to say goodbye and to wish you luck."

The handshake was firm. Garnett hoped it was a good omen. As he was leaving the vestry, he paused and said, "I wonder, what sort of a sermon do you think you will preach on Sunday, padre?"

He did not get an answer but then he hadn't expected one. The choir, a collection of middle aged women, with a sprinkling of children under twelve, began to arrive as he left the church to catch the bus for Newport at the library.

152

17

Garnett left the bus in the market square and walked back down the road, turning left at the Town Hall for the central police station. He stopped outside a tobacconist's and got a packet of V Tip out of the slot machine. There was a prickly feeling in his scalp because he didn't fancy himself in the role of a Daniel in a den of lions.

The one thing which made him really nervous was this business of hoodwinking the local police, for it was an essential part of the plan to secure their co-operation without them really knowing it. And so Vickers had dreamed up this idea of fabricating a man hunt for a woman already dead—had constructed a charade as complicated as any drawing room farce for the express purpose of convincing the police that they were working hand in glove with Special Branch. And Garnett was to be the star of this two act playlet. Garnett thought it was all very well of Endicott to tell him that his cover story was perfect, but he didn't have to put it to the test.

He walked up the short flight of steps leading into the station, showed his ID card to the desk sergeant and asked to see the Duty Officer. He was taken into a small office with green distempered walls, and introduced to a heavily built man with iron grey hair. A military type moustache decorated the upper lip and the voice was definitely plummy. The man said he was Inspector McGrath.

Garnett said, "I'm Lieutenant Commander Dayton. I believe you're expecting me?"

He had hoped that the Duty Officer would be an average run of the mill type, who was not blessed with an inquisitive and suspicious mind. His luck was right out: he had drawn a budding Napoleon. McGrath had cold grey eyes to go with the hair, and an insolent, hostile manner. He stared at Garnett while he stretched out a hairy hand and picked up a file from the In-Tray.

"Your identity card," he said curtly.

Garnett placed it on the desk and then sat down.

"The photographs don't match up, Commander."

"I beg your pardon?"

"I have a photograph of you on this file which doesn't match up with the one on your identity card."

Garnett lit a cigarette. "The trouble with official photographs," he said casually, "is that they never look right. My passport photograph, for instance, closely resembles the picture you have of Frank Arkle on the wall behind you. I see he is wanted for robbery with violence."

McGrath said, "We are talking about you, Commander, not Frank Arkle. I'm afraid I shall have to detain you, unless of course you would like to give me the name of your controller?"

That was the last thing Garnett wanted to do. It meant having implicit faith in Endicott's homework, which was something he was already beginning to doubt. He chose to avoid the suggestion.

"You've got two of my men here," he said, "have you detained them?"

"No, I haven't, but then their papers were in order."

"And mine are not?"

"Let's say I am not satisfied."

He was about to suggest that McGrath sent for Halliday and Markham to vouch for him but at the last minute he changed his mind. McGrath wanted to know the name of his controller, and it suddenly occurred to Garnett that no experienced police officer asked that sort of a question unless he had a good reason. Perhaps, despite what he said, McGrath was not altogether satisfied about Markham and Halliday. Somewhat reluctantly, Garnett decided he would have to put his faith in Endicott after all.

Garnett said, "My Controller is Colonel Robert Malone." He watched McGrath reach for the phone, and then played his ace, "You won't be able to get in touch with him; Malone has had a stroke. Nobody is supposed to know about that."

McGrath trumped his ace. He lifted the phone, asked for an outside line and then dialled his number. After a short pause,

154

McGrath said, "This is Bull Durham, am switching to secure." He punched the scrambler button and went on, "I want to speak to Colonel Malone, please."

Garnett was prepared to bet that that was one of the few times in his life when McGrath had said "please". It didn't do him much good. Garnett could see, from the expression on his face, that, in just mentioning Malone's name, McGrath had run into trouble.

His face white with anger, McGrath pushed the phone across the desk at Garnett and said, "Here, you speak to them, they won't have anything to do with me."

Garnett picked up the phone. His mouth felt dry and there was a sinking feeling in his stomach. He cleared his throat and said, "This is Blue Jay. I regret the breach of security but it is necessary to confirm my identity. Please tell the caller about Jack Daw's illness."

He handed the phone back to McGrath and waited for the fireworks. He was not disappointed. McGrath got himself cut down to size, and Garnett felt kindly disposed towards Endicott, at least for the time being.

McGrath looked up from the desk and handed the phone back to Garnett. "They want to speak to you again," he said in a subdued voice.

A voice in Garnett's ear said, "What the hell are you doing in that part of the world, Blue Jay?"

Garnett licked his lips. "I'm on to a big fish," he said in a muffled voice, "and I hope to land it very shortly. I'll call you back via this link tomorrow, okay?"

The voice said; "All right, but make sure you do not poach on Russian territory."

Garnett said okay and hung up. McGrath was toying with a retractable ball point pen, and looked a good deal less truculent.

"I was just doing my job, Commander," he said plaintively, "that's what happens to you when you are conscientious."

Garnett ignored the complaint. He said, "I'd like my men to report outside with the car. I shall also want to join your radio net; what frequency should I use?"

McGrath said; "Forty-seven megacycles, Commander, and use call

155

sign Romeo One."

"Thank you," said Garnett, "you've been most helpful; I expect you will be hearing from me again."

He stubbed out his cigarette in the brass ashtray on McGrath's desk and then left. Three minutes later, Halliday drew up outside the front entrance in a black Zephyr, and Garnett got in beside him. Markham was sitting in the back.

"Where to?" said Halliday.

"Shanklin. Just go straight on, I'll show you the way." He turned to face Markham, and said, "Have you got everything?"

"Depends what you mean by everything. We've got an FN rifle, three magazines, and a sniper scope in the boot."

"That is everything for now. Did you have any trouble?"

"Only with McGrath. I think he was suspicious."

"So?"

"So he made us wait in a special room," said Markham. "It was bugged. Halliday and I just talked about the weather."

"You did well," said Garnett. He leaned forward in his seat and twiddled the dials on the set until he had the right frequency, called up control, and got a radio check. Satisfied, he lit another cigarette and relaxed. The cold sweat under his armpits sent a chill through his body.

"I suppose you two know what you are in for?" he said.

"If we spring this man, we get a free ride out of the country, right?" Garnett nodded his head. "Good," said Markham, "that's all we're worried about."

Halliday said, "There is another reason why we are here."

"Oh yes?"

"Yes," said Halliday. "We were ordered to do it."

They turned off into a narrow road which led them through Godshill before they entered Shanklin at the top of the high street, where they turned right and went down the hill into the old village of Shanklin with its thatched roofed cottages. When they reached the Upper Chine School, Garnett told Halliday to stop the car. He picked up the radio telephone, and brushing aside all objections, told control they were closing down until the following morning.

156

Halliday said, "What's all that in aid of?"

"I don't want them to get a fix on us during the night with their radio direction finding vehicles." He smiled briefly and said, "We can move on now."

The old Saxon church was on the outskirts of Shanklin and beyond it the road climbed sharply up the landslip in a series of hairpin bends. Shortly before they reached the crest, Garnett told Halliday to put the headlights out and they then turned off the main road on to a narrow gravel track which led downhill towards the sea. The track gradually became narrower as it wound its way between giant sized blackberry bushes and overgrown hedges, until it finally petered out in a small clearing beyond a copse. Facing them was a white washed bungalow.

"Where are we?" said Markham.

"Luccomb Common. Nobody lives up here in the winter months, it's strictly for the holidaymaker. The nearest house is about three-quarters of a kilometre away."

Garnett got out of the car and walked up to the bungalow. Halliday saw him groping around the porch looking for something which he finally located under a flower pot. He opened the garage doors, stood to one side, and signalled Halliday to move the car inside. He closed the garage doors behind them, walked down the length of the Zephyr and opened a side door which led into the kitchen. Halliday and Markham got out of the car and joined him.

Garnett said; "Wait here until I have put the blackout up in the kitchen."

They heard him moving around in the kitchen and presently a dim light came on. When they stepped inside, they found Garnett on his hands and knees inside the larder. He had removed a section of the tiled floor, which was fixed on to a piece of hardboard, and had placed this makeshift trapdoor to one side. Leaning over him, Halliday found himself looking into a pit.

Garnett looked up at him and said; "I'll pass the stuff out while you two stack it on the table."

It was Pandora's Box. The cache yielded three Sterling submachine guns, nine magazines, a box containing six hundred rounds

157

of 9 mm., six chocolate brown coloured 36 grenades, three Miniman missiles, a Very pistol and two green signal cartridges, three Browning 9mm. automatics, thirty metres of polythene tubing 40mm. in diameter, thirty pounds of plastic explosive, a box of Fusee matches, two fulminate of Mercury detonators, ten metres of safety fuse, and a couple of gun cotton primers.

Markham, in an awed tone of voice, said; "My God, someone's been shopping early for Christmas."

Garnett stood up and dusted off his clothes. "Right," he said briskly, "we'll strip and clean all weapons and the grenades."

Halliday said; "I could use a drink."

"There's some coffee in the larder."

"I was thinking of something a bit stronger."

"That's your bad luck," said Garnett, "they failed to provide a bar."

He picked up a 36 grenade and unscrewed the base plug. Holding it against his chest, he removed the pin and allowed the safety lever to come off under control. The plunger thumped down the sleeve and struck him in the chest. "It works," he said with a satisfied smile.

Someone knocked on the front door.

"What the hell?" whispered Halliday.

Garnett raised a finger to his lips. The knocks were repeated, three quick and one long. Placing the grenade on the kitchen table, Garnett walked out into the hall. Markham heard a faint murmur of voices, and then Garnett came back into the room with a black man in tow.

"This is Robinson," he said quietly, "he's our Jack in the Box."

Robinson nodded at the other two men. His eyes shifted to the pile of explosives heaped up on the table. "I see you got the stuff okay," he said.

"Of course. Did you have any trouble getting here?"

"No. I came by the beach, I didn't see anyone around." Robinson's face broke into a huge smile, "But it wouldn't have mattered if there had been anyone about, people have difficulty in seeing me in the dark, man."

18

A thick sea mist hung over the Common making it impossible to see more than ten metres ahead. Halliday sat hunched over the wheel, peering through the windscreen, as he inched the car forward up the gravel track which led up to the Ventnor Road. Garnett sat beside him with the window lowered on his side, one ear cocked for approaching traffic. Somewhere out at sea, a ship blasted an uneasy warning.

Markham said, "This mist isn't going to help us."

"It's local," said Garnett, "sometimes it rolls up in the evening, other times you get it first thing in the morning. It will clear when we drop down into Shanklin. It will be another hot stinking day, you mark my words."

A wheel dropped into a pot hole. Halliday's foot slipped on the accelerator and the car bounced out of the hole, jolting them backwards and forwards against the restraint of the safety belts.

"I wouldn't care to be Robinson," said Halliday. "He must be getting a rough ride in the boot." He paused and then said, "Anything coming up on us from the left?"

Garnett said, "You're clear to come out, and take it easy, we've got plenty of time in hand. Don't turn it into a race the moment you find you have a clear view."

It occurred to Garnett he was getting jumpy. Halliday knew exactly what was required of him. He was a cool, tough and reliable man and had a Distinguished Conduct Medal to prove it. He was the last man to need anyone looking over his shoulder.

The curtain of mist ended abruptly at the outskirts of Shanklin Old Village just as Garnett had said it would. Now the sun blazed down from an almost cloudless blue sky, making the thatched

159

roofed buildings and bare trees stand out in sharp relief.

"You were right about the weather," said Markham, "must be the expert local knowledge you acquired when you were doing bird."

"Is that what passes for wit in your part of the world?" Garnett said belligerently.

In a weary voice, Halliday said, "Knock it off, you'll get all the fighting you can stomach in the next hour or so."

He was right about that, thought Garnett. He lit a cigarette and immediately wished he hadn't. His mouth was dry and his tongue had a coating of fur, and the first lungful of smoke made him feel sick. He squashed the cigarette in the ashtray, and opened his window again to allow the smoke to clear away. He noticed that they were passing the war memorial in Lake.

Garnett flicked the radio on, and picked up the tail end of a report on a traffic accident. He waited for a break in transmission and then said, "Zero, this is Romeo One, Radio check, over."

A cool female voice said, "Romeo One, okay, over."

Garnett moistened his lips. "Romeo One, on patrol, moving towards Woolworth's in Sandown High Street to pick up suspect. Suspect is Janet Prentice, I say again, Janet Prentice. Roger so far?"

McGrath came on the air and acknowledged the message. He sounded excited and breathless, as though, having heard part of the message on the monitor, he had come running into control and had snatched the mike out of the controller's hand.

Garnett said, "Suspect is described as having black hair, height five six and one half, weight one thirty-five, wearing cord slacks, black sweater and carrying plastic shoulder bag. Suspect is armed. Request stops are positioned on Brading, Lake and Yaverland roads. Will keep you informed. Acknowledge."

McGrath said, "Suggest you require assistance to make arrest."

"Negative," said Garnett.

"He won't wear that," said Halliday, "he wants to be in on the act."

"If you put your foot down, we will be there before he can get a squad car on the scene."

Halliday didn't need any urging. He swung the car into Station

160

Road, crossed the top of Fitzroy Street, slowed up at the T-junction just beyond the Queen's Cinema and then turned right into the High Street. He pulled across the road and slid into the kerb in front of Woolworth's.

"All right," said Garnett, "this is it. Let's make it look good." He got out of the car and went into the store. Halliday and Markham followed him.

There were about a dozen people in the store but even so he had difficulty in picking Dane out on the first glance. And then he saw her at the back of the shop by the hardware counter. They had cropped her hair and dyed it black but there was nothing they could do about her complexion. Prentice had had a dark swarthy skin, and even allowing for the fact that few people looked like their photograph on the wanted list, he couldn't see Dane fooling a trained interrogator for a minute. His faith in Endicott took another nose dive.

She saw him about the same time and for a moment he thought she was going to make a run for it which was not in the script, but then she appeared to change her mind and her right hand slipped inside the bag and came out with a Luger.

The first shot ploughed into a cash register just in front of Garnett, and, as he hit the floor, he thought she being too damn realistic. Glancing back over his shoulder, Garnett saw that Halliday and Markham had also gone to ground and were now working their way round the counter to cover the centre aisle. He started inching his way forward. He made about ten metres before he bobbed up, squeezed off a couple of shots and then ducked down again, as Dane returned the fire with interest.

Twelve people can make a lot of noise when they are frightened, and these people were very frightened. A fat woman crawled up the aisle towards him with her hat perched askew over one eye. Her mouth was working overtime but her screams were the silent kind. She clutched at his ankle as he crawled past her and he had to kick her quite hard to free his leg.

The building magnified the sound of each gun shot so that it sounded like a howitzer; bits of plaster, like snowflakes, drifted down from the ceiling and splinters of wood buzzed wasplike through the air. A woman crouching protectively over a child in a push chair swore at him as he went by. Garnett felt like swearing too; Dane was overdoing the realism.

He had crawled forward all of twenty-five metres before he saw Dane in a gap between the counters. She was standing sideways on to him while she fired at Halliday and Markham, and at that precise moment she ran out of ammunition. As she stooped down to change magazines, Garnett hurled himself round the counter and chopped the gun out of her hand. He slammed her back against the counter, hit her above the left eye with the butt of his automatic and then hooked her legs out from under her, before she had a chance to recover her balance. It was pure reflex action on his part.

Markham dashed forward, grabbed hold of Dane's arms, twisted them up behind her back and held them there until Halliday handcuffed her wrists together. Garnett bent down, caught Dane under one arm and lifted her to her feet.

She shook off his helping hand, and swung round to face them, her eyes blazing with anger, the blood dripping from the cut eyebrow. "Bastards, you bastards," she screamed. She lashed out with a foot and caught Garnett on the shin. The kick was painful enough to make him stagger back and clutch hold of the counter for support, and he did not see Markham sink a fist into her stomach.

Half unconscious, she was dragged out of the shop by Halliday and Markham and bundled into the back of the car. She was hardly aware of the crowd of gawking spectators on the pavement, and, afterwards when she came to think about it, Dane could only vaguely recall that Garnett had manhandled a press photographer who had got in his way. Her brain refused to function properly and her sight was blurred. A blue light was flashing and it was some time before she realised that a police car had drawn up in front of them. Garnett seemed to be excited, judging by the way he waved his arms around, and she assumed he was finding it difficult to shake off their attentions. Hunched up on the back seat beside Markham, the handcuffs biting painfully into her wrists, and her head splitting, Dane no longer gave a damn about the outcome of the argument.

162

Garnett got in beside Halliday and slammed the door. "We'd better get out of here fast," he said, "they are too officious for my liking."

"And mine," said Halliday. He took off in second and was in third inside ten metres weaving through the traffic as if he had been used to Le Mans all his life.

A harsh voice said, "Romeo One, this is Zero, confirm you have Prentice and are conforming to Sierra Oscar Papa."

Halliday said, "What the hell is Sierra Oscar Papa?"

"Jargon for Standing Operating Procedures."

"So what the hell do we do?"

"I don't know," said Garnett, "they forgot to tell me." He picked up the hand mike and said, "Romeo One, am proceeding to Parkhurst with the prisoner."

The harsh voice said, "Roger Romeo One, that is Sierra Oscar Papa."

Markham said, "I thought you expected an argument about taking her direct to Parkhurst?"

"I did," said Garnett.

"Well, I don't like it, it smells fishy to me."

And to me, Garnett thought. He wondered how Endicott had come to overlook that point in his briefing.

Dane said, "My head is splitting and my eye hurts like hell. Did you have to hit me so hard?"

Garnett reached inside his pocket and brought out a small bottle of smelling salts. "Here," he said, "try this, it might do your headache some good."

Dane leaned forward and inhaled. "That's better," she said, "now do something about my eye."

"I can't," he said. "That cut eye is the best life insurance you'll get today. It will help to take their mind off the fact that, for my money, you don't look like Prentice one little bit."

"Thanks," she said, "you've made me feel heaps better already."

Garnett ignored her. He took the Browning 9mm. automatic out of the shoulder holster and removed the magazine from the butt. Reaching forward into the glove compartment, he brought out a

163

carton of shells and methodically reloaded the magazine until it held eleven rounds. He almost fed in a twelfth until, remembering he already had one in the breech, he was superstitious enough not to tempt providence. He tapped the magazine home and slipped the Browning back into the holster.

Without a word, Halliday took one hand off the wheel, fumbled for his gun and dropped it into Garnett's lap. Mechanically he reloaded it and gave it back to Halliday and then passed the box of ammunition back over his head to Markham.

They were moving along the Newport Road now, the car purring quietly at a steady fifty. The windscreen reflected the glare of the sun and it was uncomfortably hot inside the car. Garnett lowered his window as far as it would go and leaned sideways in his seat to catch the cooling slipstream. He could hear Markham charging his magazine and each click of a round being pushed home set his nerves on edge. It seemed an age before Markham handed the carton back.

Nobody said a word. Garnett drummed his fingers on the dashboard and checked his wristwatch from time to time because he could think of nothing else to do. He glanced sideways at Halliday and saw the perspiration running down his face and thought how white he looked. He knew just how he felt, his own jaws ached from clenching his teeth together.

Garnett cleared his throat and said, "Not much further now, four kilometres or so at the most . . ." His voice tailed away. He could just make out the figure of a Russian infantryman standing in the road some eight hundred metres ahead, and as they drew closer, there was no mistaking the fact that he wanted them to slow down.

"I don't like this," Halliday muttered. "I don't like it at all."

He eased his foot off the accelerator and touched the footbrake lightly. The Russian continued to flap his arms up and down vigorously. When they were less than seventy-five metres apart, a motor cycle combination came out of a side road and took station in front of the Zephyr. A second motor cycle and sidecar fell in behind them and the sentry signalled them to move on.

Markham said, "What the hell?"

"It's all right," Garnett said as calmly as he could, "they have

164

given us an escort. At least we shall get a clear run through Newport."

In the upstairs bay window of a Victorian semi-detached house on the Cowes Road, a man kept watch. Nobody had told him that the Zephyr would have an escort of Russian security guards, and the fact that it did alarmed him. Despite his misgivings, he nevertheless passed the word over the mitre radio set and then went downstairs to make a phone call.

Further up the road, two men were lying in the loft of a similar house. They had removed a tile from the roof just above the guttering so that they had a clear view of the hospital which now served as a barracks for the Russian security battalion. As the cavalcade passed below them, one man raised the top cover of the general purpose machine gun and the other lined up the belt over the feed tray. The first man snapped the cover back in place and cocked the gun.

Three minutes later and almost four thousand metres away, two men came out of a farmhouse and walked across the yard towards the chicken run. They unlatched the gate and went inside. One of them stooped down and picked up a piece of six by four board which lay on the ground and threw it to one side. Both men then dropped down into the concealed mortar pit.

In the back garden of a terraced house less than five hundred metres from the east wall of Parkhurst, another two men crouched beside a wombat and carefully removed the bricks in the garden wall which they had loosened during the previous night. The loophole not only gave them an excellent view of the two watch towers, but also afforded a clear field of fire for the wombat.

19

The prison was a grey mass of concrete slabs, the effect of which was to lower the inmates' spirit of resistance to the point of despair. After six months inside, the prisoner became as grey and as lifeless as his surroundings. There were no windows in the four main cell blocks, and the prisoner only saw the light of day during the brief exercise period, when his horizon was limited by the forbidding perimeter walls, and the death wire which marked the edge of the minefield.

Halliday drew up outside the Reception block and cut the engine. The tail escort had peeled off at the entrance to the prison but the leading motor cycle and sidecar had stayed with them and was now parked a few metres in front of the Zephyr.

"The buggers are not going to move," Halliday said quietly.

Garnett said, "You will have to deal with them before you let Robinson out of the boot. Watch the sentry on the gate, he could be dangerous."

He got out of the car and opened the rear door. Reaching inside, Garnett grabbed hold of Dane and jerked her out of the car and then pushed her towards the entrance of the block. From the expression on their faces, his rough handling of Dane seemed to meet with the approval of the Russian escorts.

The layout inside the block was exactly as Taylor had described it. A Russian sentry was standing on the left of the door cradling a 7.62mm. Shpagin M1941 PPSH sub machine gun in his arms, and two British warders manned the counter which both spanned the width of the room, and prevented further progress into the building beyond that point.

The elder of the two warders was a fat sergeant who had a kindly

166

face and a jovial expression to go with it. Considering what his job entailed, Garnett thought he had about as much appeal as did Uriah Heap. His companion was younger, more agile, fitter and, judging by the narrowness of his eyes, probably twice as mean.

The sergeant said; "Well, well, so this is Janet Prentice is it?" He rubbed his hands together as though he was washing them under a tap. "I see you've messed her up a bit, but that will be nothing compared to the treatment she'll get from our Hilda and Alice." He reached out with a soft, plump hand and pinged the bell on the counter.

Two women emerged from the back office. They were without doubt the most unprepossessing creatures Garnett had ever seen. The taller of the two was over six feet and almost as broad. Her breasts sagged to meet her stomach and she waddled like a duck. Her eyes were small blackcurrants sunk in a mountain of pudgy grey flesh, the legs were miniature tree trunks and the hands resembled slabs of raw meat. Her black hair was drawn back in a tight bun behind her neck and tied in place with a piece of blue ribbon. In comparison, her friend looked half her size because she was shaped like a plank. A hatchet face, and mouse coloured hair which had suffered a crew cut, emphasised her masculine appearance.

The sergeant grinned at the fat woman and said, "She's all yours, Hilda." He raised the counter flap, simpered at Dane, and said, "Come inside."

Garnett said, "You haven't signed for her yet."

The sergeant scrawled his signature across a blank committal form and handed it to Garnett. "Will this do you?" he sneered.

"I want to see the governor." The sergeant raised one eyebrow questioningly. "This prisoner has vital information," said Garnett, "she must be interrogated as soon as possible."

"I know," said the sergeant. "That's why Hilda and Alice are here. They'll sweat it out of her."

"I still want to see the governor."

"You'll have to wait then. The governor is in conference with the general. If you are going to wait, I suggest you check your gun in with me now, it will save time later."

167

Garnett didn't hear a word he said. His attention was riveted on Dane. The two freaks had propped her up at an angle so that her head was resting against the wall, while her legs were splayed apart. They were, he supposed, searching her in case she had secreted a suicide pill on her person. It was a job which left plenty of scope for their peculiar mentality and they made the most of it, pawing her breasts and stroking her abdomen, and Dane had to stand there and take it because he was powerless to intervene. He wondered if Dane hated him for what they were doing to her.

"You will have to leave your gun with me, Commander," the sergeant said again.

"What?" Garnett said vaguely.

"It's the rule, nobody is allowed to take a weapon into the governor's office."

It's a balls up, Garnett thought. The fisherman has failed to produce the goods, and now there were but two choices; they could either go it alone without outside help, or he could abandon Dane and bluff his way out which would at least save Markham, Halliday and Robinson. Neither proposition appealed to him. He glanced at Markham standing beside him and saw the sweat running down his face, and knew he would soon have to come to a decision. Reluctantly he slipped the Browning out of the shoulder holster and laid it on the counter.

"I want a receipt for it," he said.

His hand was still hovering over the butt when he heard the tinkle of shattered glass. The whole building seemed to rock on its foundations and then the thunderclap broke.

Garnett snatched up the automatic. "It came from outside," he shouted to the bewildered desk sergeant.

He whirled round and shot the Russian sentry through the back of the neck. The man grunted and buckled at the knees just the way cattle in the slaughter house do when the humane killer slams into the brain.

And, just as he had expected, the opposition's reaction was slow. The sergeant was staring bug eyed at his companion who was crawling round the floor in circles, with the lower half of his jaw

168

shot away. He was still fumbling to get his pistol out of the holster when Garnett shot him twice in the stomach. He sank down on to his knees and his head dropped forward so that he looked like a Mohammedan in prayer. Markham leaned over the counter and casually shot the man who had only half of his face left.

Hilda started screaming but still had the presence of mind to grab hold of Dane and use her as a human shield. The third warder came out of the inner office waving a gun above his head, saw Markham and Garnett and tried to run back inside. Hit repeatedly in the back, he slid down the length of the door frame leaving a bloody smear on the white paintwork.

Enfolded in the arms of a mountain of sour smelling flesh, Dane was swept off her feet. Unable to get leverage from the floor, she scraped the heel of her shoe down the length of Hilda's leg from kneecap to shin. The pain was such that momentarily Hilda relaxed her hold, and Dane was able to touch the floor, sag at the knees and then spring up again, her head catching Hilda under the chin with the force of a pile driver.

Finding herself completely free, Dane whirled round and kicked the dyke on the kneecap. Hilda screamed in agony and fell over sideways. Seeing that fat obscenity writhing on the floor, and remembering how those meaty hands had pinched her breasts and probed her crotch, Dane made no effort to control the rage within her. Quite deliberately she measured the distance and smashed the outside edge of her right foot against the exposed head.

It slowly dawned on Alice that these people would probably kill her, and stimulated by a sudden concern for her own safety, she made a dive for the shotgun which was hidden under the counter. She met the barrel of Markham's Browning on the down swing and discovered too late that her skull had no more resistance than that of an eggshell.

Garnett vaulted over the counter. Glancing back at Markham, he yelled at him to remove the handcuffs from Dane's wrists.

Halliday had been staring at the far watch tower for what seemed an eternity, steeling himself not to jump when, and if, the 120mm. wombat shell arrived on the target. He was aware that the trio of

Russian solders who were standing by the motor cycle and sidecar were talking about him. From time to time he had caught them grinning contemptuously in his direction, and their attitude made him angry. By moving his knee upwards a fraction, he could feel the Sterling sub machine gun in the rack beneath the instrument panel, and derived satisfaction from the thought that in a very short space of time he would wipe the smile from their faces.

He was beginning to believe that the attack would never get off the ground, when suddenly the machine gun post on top of the tower disintegrated. Slabs of concrete rained down into the compound but despite this advanced warning, he was completely unprepared for the violence of the explosion. The car seemed to momentarily lose contact with the ground as a result of the shock wave set up by the explosive energy.

Halliday recovered his wits, grabbed the Sterling and fired a burst through the windscreen. The zone toughened glass became a crazy mosaic reducing vision to nil, until he punched a hole through it with his fist. He emptied the rest of the magazine into the three Russians, of whom not a single one managed to load his weapon much less return the fire. Halliday changed magazines, pulled the quick release gear which triggered the trunk, and slid out of the car.

Robinson had heard the burst of gun fire and was puzzled by it. He had been prepared for an explosion but the small arms fire was totally unexpected. For a brief second or so, he was inclined to think that the Russians had reacted more quickly than they had anticipated. Whatever doubts he had immediately disappeared when the lid of the trunk sprang open.

Clutching the Miniman projectiles in either hand, he flung himself out of the boat and landed heavily on his shoulder. The need for quick reaction produced near farcical results. He found himself trying to point the wrong end of the Miniman at the guardroom, and, hastily correcting the error, he became so keyed up that the first missile went high and struck the gable, lifting a great chunk out of the roof. He threw the first launcher aside and grabbed hold of another one.

He was aware that Halliday was standing to his right and rear,

170

engaging the sentry with single shot. He had just lined up the second missile on to the target, when a hot, empty cartridge case fell on to the calf of his left leg, where the trousers had rucked up to expose the bare flesh. The sudden burning sensation made him jump at the critical moment, and the rocket missed the guardroom altogether. His third shot was however right on target.

The first explosion had killed the four men who were lying on their beds just inside the entrance to the guardroom, and so dazed the remainder that they were incapable of moving quickly. The final round produced an overkill. The remaining thirty-two men died from the combined effects of blast and the fragmentation of the concrete structure which produced a hail of chippings, which travelled through the air with bullet like velocity.

Scrambling to his feet, Robinson reached inside the boot for the explosive tubing and the Very pistol, and found himself being jostled by Halliday who was trying to grab the FN rifle and the pouch containing two spare magazines. They pushed and shoved each other out of the way, like two women fighting over a bargain in the January sales, spurred on by the machine gun fire which was now coming their way from one of the towers on the west wall.

Garnett started moving up the staircase which led to the prison governor's office. He was about halfway up, when the door at the top of the stairs opened, and the Russian bodyguard appeared. Instinctively Garnett crouched down and fired three shots in rapid succession. The Russian, hit in the left shoulder, chest, and face, pitched head first down the stairs taking Garnett along with him.

The Russian was a big man by any standard and the dead weight of his body which pinned Garnett to the floor felt all of two hundred pounds in weight. Garnett eased his way out from underneath the dead man, and, pausing only to remove a stick grenade from the leather belt around the Russian's waist, started to make his way back up the staircase.

Someone had closed the door at the top of the stairs and was now firing the odd shot through it to discourage callers. Garnett was forced to work his way forward on his stomach until his head was just below the level of the top step. It seemed there was no way of opening the door which didn't invite self destruction, and he was still trying to think of a solution to the problem when the building shuddered again as the second tower on the east wall was hit. The explosion presented him with the opportunity he needed. Leaping to his feet, Garnett unlatched the door and threw it open and was then forced to drop flat, as round after round buzzed over his head like a disturbed swarm of bees.

Garnett looked at the stick grenade in his hand and debated whether or not to pull out the pin before he threw it into the office. The trouble was that he didn't know how long the damn thing took to go off. If he threw it too soon, they would have enough time to pick it up and lob it back at him; and if he held on to it for a few seconds there was a chance it would blow up in his face. He decided to chuck the grenade inside without removing the pin since it would probably catch them off-guard for that vital second or so when he came charging into the room.

In the event he was more than just lucky; Providence was definitely on his side and working overtime. Both men had dived behind their desks for cover when they saw the grenade arch into the room and were still crouching there waiting for it to go off when Garnett entered.

Hero of the Soviet Union, Major General Igor Vishinsky was shot and killed while still on his hands and knees. Governor Laker, a tiny man, lay on his stomach with his hands clapped over his ears passively awaiting execution. He survived because in the end Garnett didn't have the stomach to kill him. Instead he bent down and clubbed Laker with the butt of his automatic, an act of mercy which he would later come to regret.

Dane took one look at the carnage around her and then made her way up to the governor's office before she vomited. She crouched beside Garnett at the window and peered at the machine gunners in the towers on the west wall.

Garnett said, "All right, you've seen them, now start picking them off."

"With what?" she said, fingering the congealed blood on her cheekbone. "I haven't got the rifle. I'm still waiting for Halliday to

172

give it to me."

Halliday was lying behind the Zephyr with Robinson, seeking protection from the hail of machine gun fire. He had calculated the distance from his position to the comparative safety of Reception and weighed his chances of covering the fifteen metres in the open and had concluded they were zero. He knew it was vital to get the rifle to Dane, but he couldn't see how he could manage it without getting himself killed before he reached the entrance.

He could hear a solid whunk, as bullet after bullet punctured the car body and he wondered how long it would be before a tracer round ignited the petrol in the tank. He found out soon enough. The tank exploded in a great gout of flame which sent rivulets of burning petrol snaking across the tarmac. Black smoke belched upwards, making it difficult for the machine gunners to see their target.

Halliday was the first to realise that the burning petrol was providing them with a ready made smoke screen. He leapt to his feet, and carrying the FN rifle and ammunition pouch in one hand and the Sterling sub machine gun in the other, made a frantic dash for the entrance to Reception. After a moment's hesitation Robinson followed his example. As he dived inside the building after Halliday, he saw a scab of concrete fly off from the base of the wall midway between the two shattered watch towers.

Garnett scanned the compound anxiously. The flames and smoke from the burning Zephyr obscured his vision as much as it hampered the Russians'. If Vickers was correct, there were eight prowler sentries somewhere and so far he had not sighted one. It was possible they were inside the cell blocks but he rather doubted that. His eyes flicked towards the prison gates where at any moment he expected the reinforcements to come streaming in from the barracks across the road. Above the noise of the wombat, it was hard to judge whether or not the fisherman had got the mortar and the machine guns into action.

Halliday came flying into the room and dropped down beside Dane. He was out of breath and for a few seconds he was unable to speak, not that words were necessary. Dane snatched the FN out of his hands, and cocked it slickly. She checked the telescopic sight and

173

was just coming up into the aim when a series of explosions ripped the Zephyr apart and shattered the window in front of her face. By a miracle she escaped injury.

Garnett said, "Christ, what was that?"

"The hand grenades," Halliday said lamely, "I left them behind."

"What else did you forget?"

"The other two Sterlings."

Garnett looked him up and down. He counted slowly to ten and then said, "I wonder you didn't join the other side while you were at it."

The explosion had one beneficial effect. It virtually snuffed out the fire and enabled Dane to focus the telescopic sight on the nearest tower. She had the crosswires over the machine gunner's chest and then hesitated. Shooting down falling plates was one thing, a man was quite another. She lowered the rifle and rubbed her good eye.

Garnett leaned towards her. "Shoot," he said. His voice was quiet but insistent.

She brought the butt up into her shoulder again, and, closing her mind to the consequences, took aim and squeezed the trigger. Scarcely waiting to see the result, she tracked on to the next target and fired again. She silenced both machine guns with five rounds.

Prison Governor Laker stirred and gingerly touched the back of his head and found that his hand came away sticky with blood. Without really knowing why, he dragged himself to his feet, bent over the desk and, screaming into the intercom, told the guards to gas the prisoners. It was unnecessary and it cost him his life. As he lay dying, Laker recalled bitterly that the guards had standing orders to gas the prisoners if a mass escape was attempted.

Halliday lowered his Sterling and glared at Garnett. "Did you hear that?" he said. "You should have killed him before when you had the chance."

"So I made a mistake," said Garnett. "Let's hope they are not using nerve gas." He turned away and touched Dane lightly on her shoulder. "Watch out for the prowler sentries and keep an eye on the gate. I don't want any interference coming from the barracks across the road." He got to his feet and ran downstairs.

174

Markham was examining a rifle which he had discovered in the armoury inside the inner office. An identical model lay on the counter in front of him. He looked up as Garnett entered the room and said, "What do you make of this?"

Garnett said, "It's an Armelite 5.56mm. Did you find any ammunition to go with it?"

"A couple of magazines."

Garnett picked up the Armelite on the counter and loaded it. "Set it for single shot like so," he said, "because twenty rounds on automatic won't last more than a couple of seconds."

He moved to the entrance and crouched down beside Robinson. "You okay?" he asked.

Robinson patted the coil of explosive tubing lying at his side. "Sure, ready to go when you are."

"I'll take the Very pistol, then."

Robinson slipped his arm out of the harness and passed the holster to Garnett. A sudden rushing noise made him jump. "What was that?" he said.

"Incoming mail." The ripple of explosions convinced Garnett that the mortar was giving rapid instead of deliberate fire as he had asked. He looked back at Markham and Halliday and said, "We haven't got much time, so let's get our sprinting shoes on." He shot out of the door and started running towards the prison hospital in the centre of the compound.

The 81mm. mortar crew had reached a private agreement. They were supposed to put down intermittent fire but in their opinion this was taking an unnecessary risk. The longer they remained in action, the more chance the Russians had of pinpointing their location by radar. They planned therefore to get rid of the ammunition as swiftly as possible in case the radar picked up the bombs in flight and computed their position on the ground. To speed things up, they stood on either side of the mortar, and took it in turn to drop a bomb down the tube. Their drill was slick; unfortunately by the eleventh bomb it was altogether too slick. They achieved a double load and the resultant premature explosion peeled open the mortar barrel like a banana, killing both men

175

instantly.

The machine gunners in the loft of the house had a good view of the hospital barracks. They were, if anything, somewhat surprised by the slow reaction of the Russians. For some minutes after the wombat had opened fire on the watch towers, nothing had happened in the hospital area. They were beginning to think that they were an unnecessary luxury when they noticed signs of activity near the entrance to the hospital barracks. A few seconds later, a group of men tried to rush across the road towards the prison. The machine gunner cut them down with a long burst of twenty-five rounds. The vibrating effect of the general purpose machine gun raised a cloud of dust inside the loft and the second man was obliged to dampen the floor boards with a ladle of water in order that they should be able to see their target clearly.

Three times, the Russians tried to scuttle across the road and each time they met with failure. The fourth time round, they got wise. They threw a phosphorous smoke grenade before they started running.

Robinson stood by the death wire which marked the outer edge of the minefield and studied the problem facing him. The hole blasted in the wall was wide enough for a big man to pass through without too much difficulty, providing he ducked his head at the right moment. The difficulty lay in blowing a path through the minefield right up to the hole.

Whirling thirty metres of explosive tubing around and releasing it so that it fell in the right place was going to be a chancy business, because here and there he could see the prongs of an anti-personnel mine sticking up out of the loose earth. It required little imagination to picture what would happen if the tubing should hit one of the exposed prongs. He could only hope that the impact of the tubing on a concealed mine would be less than the pressures exerted by a man treading on the surface above the mine.

Robinson licked his lips, offered up a silent prayer, and began to whirl the tubing above his head, paying it out like a cowboy performing with a lariat. Still retaining hold of one end, he released the tubing and closed his eyes. The dull plopping sound as the tube

176

fell harmlessly to earth was almost an anticlimax.

He could scarcely believe his eyes when he saw that the tubing had landed within a metre of the hole. He fished the detonator and safety fuse out of his pocket and inserted it into the primer. Hands shaking like leaves in the wind, he struck a Fusee match, lit the safety fuse, and then walked briskly towards the shelter of the Reception Block.

A sharp blow on the back knocked Robinson off balance. Glancing down at his chest, he saw pieces of shattered bone around the lip of a gaping hole the size of a tea cup. It slowly dawned on him that he had been shot. One foot became entangled with the other and he lurched towards the death wire. In that split second before final oblivion he called out his wife's name as he toppled on to the waiting prongs of a shoe mine. Seconds after the shoe mine had blown up underneath Robinson, the explosive tubing opened up a zigzag lane through the minefield.

Legs pumping like pistons, his head lolling from side to side, Garnett sprinted across the four hundred metres of open ground leading to the hospital. At the three hundred metre mark his limbs felt as heavy as lead, there was a tight pain in his chest and he saw the building in a blur. With fifty metres to go, he thought he wasn't going to make it, and he could hear Markham and Halliday closing up on him. He had gone out too fast, failed to pace himself correctly and had burnt up his energy too soon. When he reached the entrance to the hospital, he was obliged to lean against the wall until he regained his breath.

Garnett tried the double doors of the hospital and found them locked. If he hadn't been under such intense pressure, the flimsy nature of the doors might have puzzled him. As it was he merely saw them as an obstacle which had to be dealt with as quickly as possible. Signalling Markham to do likewise, he backed off several paces and then came at the doors fast, hitting them below the lock with the point of his right shoulder. Garnett survived because he hit them a fraction ahead of Markham, and when they gave way he went sprawling on the slippery floor inside.

Markham managed to keep his balance by jumping over Garnett, but, before he could stop himself, he cannoned into a steel grill. The impact winded him and he hung on to the bars with one hand while he collected his wits. The Russian sentry standing at the far end of the corridor shot him to pieces from the crutch to the throat.

Forgetting everything he had said, Garnett switched the Armelite on to automatic and emptied the magazine in one long frantic burst as he lay on the floor, shattering the drug cabinet, smashing the glass windows in the treatment room and almost cutting the Russian in half from the waist up.

To have got this far and then to find that all that stood between him and success was a lousy stinking gate was an unbelievably cruel stroke of luck. Dragging himself to his feet, Garnett smashed the Armelite against the lock again and again, until the stock and butt disintegrated along with his pent up rage and frustration. Close to despair he threw the shattered rifle away, and, grabbing hold of the grating with both hands, shook the gate impotently.

A sudden tinkle made him look down and he saw the key lying on the floor where it had fallen from the lock, and he realised that the sentry had forgotten to remove it when he had locked the gate. Bending down, he thrust his hand through the bars and scooped up the precious key.

Halliday had remained outside the hospital to keep an eye on the area behind the cell blocks which Dane could not see from her vantage point. He licked his lips repeatedly and glanced anxiously about him. Garnett had warned him about the guard dogs, and he was worried because there was a chance that he might not hear one approach him above all the noise until it was almost too late.

A sixth sense made the hairs on his neck stand up, and whirling round, he was just in time to see the Russian bring his automatic rifle up into the aim. They were nearly a hundred metres apart, which was much too far for the Sterling to have any real degree of accuracy but Halliday didn't have any choice. He fired a short burst of two rounds and then the gun stopped. Desperately he re-cocked it and squeezed the trigger again. The dull clunk as the bolt hit the breech told him that the magazine was empty and he cried out in despair. The note of panic died in the vomit of blood spewed up

178

from his lungs as his chest caved in.

The Russian was feeling good. This was the second man he had killed that morning and over confidence made him careless. He walked towards Halliday, forgetting that he was coming out into the open. Dane thought that she had hit him a trifle high, but in the event it didn't really matter. His steel helmet flew up into the air, and what remained of his head looked as if it had been caught in a giant press.

Garnett should have picked up Markham's rifle but in his haste he omitted to do so. Common sense should have told him that the sentry was there for a purpose but he wasn't thinking too clearly and he wasted valuable time searching the wards on either side of the corridor, before it dawned on him that the Russian had been standing guard outside the room he wanted. He stepped over the dead soldier and opened the door.

The man lying in the bed was wrestling feebly with a tough, pock-marked orderly who was trying to hold him still, so that the doctor, who had his back to Garnett, could inject him. There was no way of knowing whether the syringe was lethal or not, but at least Taylor was wrong about the nerve gas.

The orderly caught sight of Garnett as he was drawing the Very pistol from the holster. He shouted a warning and reached under his smock for the pistol he kept stuffed in the waistband of his trousers, but hampered by the hospital clothing he was a shade too slow. The signal flare buried itself into his chest and knocked him on to the floor, where he lay on his back thrashing about and screaming in agony, as he tried to pluck the wad of burning magnesium out of the wound.

The doctor grabbed a jug of water and heaved it at Garnett, catching him on the shoulder. It gave him just enough time to snatch up a pair of ugly looking surgical scissors from the tray of instruments lying on the trolley, and which he then held in front of his body as he advanced towards Garnett. Garnett managed to avoid the first lunge, and the doctor tripped over his outstretched leg. Falling violently at an acute angle, the point of the scissors was deflected backwards on contact with the floor through almost

179

ninety degrees and penetrated the abdominal cavity, killing the doctor instantly.

The patient said, "Nice of you to drop by. I'm Pollard."

"You don't look a bit like your photograph."

"That's one of the reasons why I survived so long. They've always been looking for the wrong man."

"How did they manage to identify you then?"

Pollard said, "For God's sake, are we going to stay here all day while you ask inane questions?"

"No, we aren't. Can you manage to walk out of here unaided?"

Pollard tried to sit up in bed and fell back exhausted by the effort. The dressing on his left shoulder began to turn reddish brown in one place where the wound had re-opened and started to bleed. "For pity's sake," he gasped, "can't you stop that man screaming."

"Certainly," Garnett said in a wooden voice. He walked round the bed and kicked the orderly in the head. The screams died abruptly.

Pollard said, "In the shape I am in, I'm not going to make it out of here. You'd better leave me."

Garnett said, "That's impossible. You're one of the pioneers; if you talk, two hundred and fifty men and women die."

"What the hell are you talking about?"

"You're one of the key men in the Resistance Organisation."

Pollard said, and every word was an effort, "I work under Vickers in the Operations Branch. I planned Blythe's assassination with a little help from Security and Intelligence but I wasn't even supposed to carry out the job. A man called Abrahams was, but he got himself knocked down and killed in an accident three days before it was due to come off and I took his place without telling anyone."

Pollard broke off in a coughing fit. The sputum on his lips was flecked with blood. "Forget about the two hundred and fifty. If I talk, only Vickers, Endicott and Coleman will get hurt. The fact that the Special Branch had me brought here is just routine; if anyone told you different, you've been had."

Garnett said, "All right, so I've been had, but having come this far I'm not leaving without you. I'm going to tie your wrists together,

180

loop them over my head, and drag you out of here on my back."

When the alarm bells sounded, Taylor was patrolling the lower sub floor of Block Two, supervising a detail of four prisoners who were scrubbing out the urinal buckets they had collected from the cells. Although he had sensed there was something in the air after his meeting with Garnett, he had not expected an attack to be made on the prison. Not that it made the slightest difference to his attitude because Taylor had no intention of becoming involved. He donned a respirator and waving his nightstick, signalled the prisoners to get back into their cells quietly.

He had never experienced anything but unquestioning obedience, and it never occurred to him that one day the prisoners might turn on him. Three men on the detail were in no hurry to get themselves gassed and feeling vexed, Taylor walked briskly towards them, completely forgetting that he had turned his back on the fourth man.

The latrine bucket caught Taylor behind the knees and bowled him over. Before he could get up, the four men pounced on him and one of them clapped a hand over the air intake filter of his respirator, cutting off the supply of oxygen. The face mask pressed against his nose as he desperately fought to get his breath. He wanted to tell them that he was on their side, but he was unable to speak and gradually he lost consciousness. Feverish hands rolled his body over and went through the pockets.

Dane kept an anxious eye on the hospital while she fought a running battle with the reinforcements coming up from the barracks. In the circumstances it was perhaps inevitable that two sharp-shooters were able to slip inside the gates, while her attention was diverted elsewhere, and take cover in the ruins of the guardroom where they lay concealed, popping up now and again to take a random shot at her.

It was hard going carrying one hundred and seventy pounds on his back, but it was a lot harder on Pollard, for each jolting stride made him cry out in agony. The dog appeared from behind Cell Block One and came full pelt at them. Unable to bring the Armelite up into his shoulder because Pollard's arms were in the way, Garnett shot repeatedly from the hip and missed. It seemed there was a good chance the dog would get him until Dane managed to drop it when it was about to leap at his throat.

Half blinded by sweat, Garnett could scarcely push one leg in front of the other. He had reached that stage of physical exhaustion where he wanted to be sick and the mind seemed to be divorced from reality. The sight of a dozen or so walking scarecrows almost convinced him that he was having hallucinations, until he realised that these shaven headed figures in ill fitting dungarees, who were milling about in the compound, were escaping prisoners. He was almost level with the Reception Block now, and he wondered what the hell was keeping Dane.

Dane crouched by the wall and peered above the window sill cautiously. A 7.62mm. Kalashnikov AKM assault rifle stuttered, gouging pockmarks in the ceiling above her head and she was forced to duck out of sight. Unless she could do something about the sharpshooters, they were going to trap her in the office. She backed away from the window, scuttled across the room like a crab and ran downstairs. Gingerly skirting the bloody shambles on the floor behind the counter, she inched her way forward to the entrance of the block.

Peering out, she was in time to see one of the sharpshooters bob up into view and heave a stick grenade across the compound. Her reflexes were still good. She shot the Russian before he had a chance to get down, and, swivelling, she caught the second man as he came up for a snap shot.

Garnett dropped the Armélite at his feet, and, taking the Very pistol out of the holster, loaded it with a green signal cartridge. As he stretched his arm above his head and fired, the stick grenade exploded twenty paces behind him. Pollard screamed and Garnett felt his left leg go numb below the calf. He was surprised to find that he could still manage to hobble forward, but despite this he knew he could not make the path through the minefield unaided. It was then that Dane arrived, and slipping his arm over her shoulder, she was able to take some of the weight off his injured leg.

Baker had expected to see two green signal flares but he wasn't going to be pedantic about it. He slammed the bonnet down, leapt

182

inside the car and gunned the engine into life. He fish-tailed the corner and was roaring down the straight when he saw two figures emerge through the gap in the East Wall and stagger out into the road. One of them appeared to be carrying someone on his back. He hit the brakes, shifted into first gear and skidded to a halt. The rear door was jerked open and two men fell inside and collapsed on to the floor in a heap. A girl with a black eye got in beside him.

Baker pressed his foot down savagely and let in the clutch. The wheels spun crazily, bit into the road and left burning particles of rubber on the surface. Shifting through the gears, he reached top in less than forty metres and coming down the hill into Newport, he broke a ton and a half.

Garnett slipped out of Pollard's embrace and, wriggling free, collapsed on to the back seat. One glance at the bloody mess at his feet was enough to convince him that Pollard was dead, and losing interest, he rolled up his trouser leg and examined the gash in his calf. The wound was bleeding far too much for his liking, and removing his tie, he used it to make a tourniquet.

Dane said, "How is he?"

"Dead," said Garnett.

For a moment or so she did not grasp the significance of what he had said, and then, as the full facts came home to her, she struck her clenched fists against the dashboard and the tears welled in her eyes and ran down her cheeks.

Houses, shops and pedestrians flashed by in a blur as Baker swung the car through the narrow streets. He handled the Jaguar as if he was a part of the machine. His judgement was superb and Garnett doubted whether any other man could have handled the car as well as what he did.

"Did you notice the decoy car wasn't there?" said Baker.

"I noticed."

"What does that mean?" Dane said anxiously.

"It means we are on our own."

Tyres screaming in protest, they turned on to the Brading Road and began to climb up on to the Downs. It really was a beautiful day, marred only by one thing. Glancing back, Garnett saw a helicopter over Newport which was heading in their direction.

20

Garnett said; "We've got company."

Baker jumped and momentarily lost control of the car which ran off the road, mounted the grass verge and bucked and jolted over the uneven surface. A branch raked the coachwork from fender to fender, smashing the offside headlight and denting the front wing. Somehow he managed to drag the car back on to the road without once reducing speed. A curious drumming noise started up and the steering wheel shuddered in Baker's hands.

"What's the matter?" Garnett shouted.

"The wing's fouling the tyre and throwing the steering out. We will strip the tread bald in next to no time."

Garnett looked out of the rear window again. The Hound helicopter was closing the distance rapidly. A few minutes ago the fact that it appeared to be heading in their direction might have been coincidence. Now it began to look as though the pilot was following instructions, and Garnett thought it was possible that some well meaning citizen had reported their movements to the police. Even as he was looking, a second Hound appeared above Newport and made off in a south-westerly direction.

"We are going to leave you at the S-bend," said Garnett, "It might throw the pilot and give you a chance." He crouched down beside the door and depressed the catch. "Slow it down to thirty before we come out of the bend."

He heard Baker change into third before he braked and he started to push the door open. The slipstream threatened to slam the door back in his face, but exerting his strength, he forced it open and threw himself out. He thought he heard Baker shouting, "Go, go, go."

Garnett hit the grass verge on his left shoulder and rolled over and over until he was finally stopped by a thick gorse bush which lacerated his hands and face. The world stopped spinning and he could hear Dane calling out to him. Crawling out of the gorse bush, he found her a few metres away, nursing the cut above her eye which had reopened. He dragged her into cover and pressed her face into the earth as the helicopter gun ship flew overhead.

The Hound came in behind the Jaguar, close enough for the pilot to identify the registration number before he put the ship into hover. His co-pilot needed at least two hundred metres to get the wire guided missile under control, so he wasn't concerned when the Jaguar began to draw away from the helicopter.

Garnett saw the missile leave the pod and slowly gather momentum. The flare from the rocket motor both fascinated and repelled him as he watched the missile home on to the car. Afterwards he could have sworn there was a dull clang, as metal made contact with metal a split second before the missile exploded. The car disintegrated before his eyes; a wheel shot up into the air high above the blazing wreckage, which was spread out over a hundred metres, and then bounced back to earth.

He could feel Dane struggling to sit up but he held her down while he waited for the Hound to make the next move. It was no good making for the Dormobile now, even supposing it was there. A second vehicle appearing from nowhere would alert the pilot and they wouldn't stand a chance. He considered the alternative escape plan which Endicott had said he could use in an emergency and decided that now was the time to make use of it.

The Hound back tracked and briefly circled the area above them, and then, apparently satisfied, the pilot turned the ship away and headed off back in the direction of Newport. A black pall of smoke hung in the air above the Jaguar.

Garnett released his hold on Dane and examined his leg which he saw was still bleeding, and he realised that if he couldn't stop it altogether, he would leave a spoor which even a blind man could follow. And even if he stopped it bleeding, there was still the problem of avoiding the search party and the tracker dogs which

185

could be expected to appear on the scene as a matter of routine. He wished now that he had thought to bring a bag of pepper along with him to put the dogs off the scent. There was only one solution and it stood out a mile. They would have to separate and he would try to lead them off in a false direction while Dane made her way to the hide. He pulled his shirt out of his trousers and hacked off a strip from the tail, which he then ripped in half, wadding up one piece as a bandage and using the other strip to tie it in place over the wound.

He saw Dane watching him curiously and he wondered if she had guessed what he was thinking. He leaned towards her and brushed the dirt off her face gently. "I want you to listen carefully," he said quietly, "just in case I cannot keep up with you. There is a hide about four kilometres from here which should be safe enough. It's in a small copse north-north-east of Brading near Downside Farm."

She tossed her head angrily. "I don't want to hear any more," she said, "either we make it together or I don't go at all. Put your arm around my shoulder and I'll get you there somehow."

He felt ashamed. Ashamed, because for a brief moment back there in the prison he had entertained the idea of abandoning Dane even if he had subsequently rejected it. Ashamed, because no such idea had occurred to her when the circumstances were reversed.

He wanted to tell her that he thought she was pretty wonderful but he couldn't find the words, he just looked at her and said, "All right honey bun, let's get started." He realised it sounded inadequate.

Her physical strength and determination surprised him. At times it felt as if she was virtually carrying him and he knew that without her help he would not have got very far. They had covered about a kilometre when they came to the brook, and at his insistence they entered it and marched downstream for nearly two kilometres before they put foot on dry land again. It was the only way he could think of to throw the dogs off their scent.

From time to time they heard the sound of helicopters in the distance, and Garnett thought it possible that the Russians were trying to establish a wide cordon. He wished them luck, the further they put the cordon out the better he liked it.

It took them nearly two hours of sheer torture to reach the hide. He had said that it was about four kilometres from their starting point, but in following the stream he had added another two. The sky had begun to darken when they finally made it, and there was a rumble of thunder in the distance. Halliday's heat wave had ended.

The hide was hollowed out under a clump of trees and measured roughly ten by six by four. It contained a stock of canned food, hexamine fuel tablets, four jerrycans of water, an Elsan of sorts, a first aid pack and a number of sleeping bags. Ventilation was adequate provided they remained inactive but in any case it was difficult to do otherwise since it was impossible to stand upright. There was of course no lighting.

Dane looked around and shivered in the damp air. "Are we likely to be here for long?" she asked.

"Ten days, maybe three weeks. It depends when they think it is safe enough to come for us."

"Perhaps they will never come. Perhaps we shall stay here until we die."

"They will come," he said firmly.

"Look," she said, holding out her hands, "See? I can't stop them shaking."

"It will pass," he said, "it's only nervous reaction."

Garnett dragged out the first aid pack and opened it. Rummaging through the contents he found some lint, a bottle of iodine, a needle and a spool of cat gut.

"What do you want that stuff for?" she asked anxiously.

"I'm going to patch up your eye."

"Oh, no you're not."

"Come on, it won't hurt."

"I've heard that one before."

He crawled towards her and began to swab the cut as gently as he could but the iodine hurt her and she sucked in her breath sharply.

"I don't want any stitches," she said faintly.

He pressed the lips of the wound together.

"You hear me? No stitches."

"All right," he said, "hand me the sticking plaster."

He snipped off a suitable length and pressed it down firmly on the wound.

"That hurt," she said.

"I'm sorry," said Garnett.

He leaned back against the earth wall and lit a cigarette. After a short pause, he said; "We may have to leave separately. I'm only hazarding a guess but you never know. In those circumstances, it might be difficult for us to meet up with one another again."

She listened to him in silence and waited for him to finish voicing his thoughts.

"I could put an advert in the press on the first of each month. Something to the effect that author engaged on writing book dealing with history of British canals requires secretary-research assistant. Salary open to negotiation but not less than fifteen hundred. Write box number and state qualifications and experience."

"And then I would apply for the job, and you would know where to find me?"

"That's roughly the idea," he said.

"I think it is a good one," she said. "Don't forget to put it into practice."

Garnett stubbed his cigarette out on the floor. "I'm afraid I will have to ask you to put some stitches into my leg."

"All right," she said, "but I ought to warn you that I've had absolutely no experience in that sort of thing. I might hurt you."

"I'll chance it," said Garnett.

The minute she started to work on his leg, he knew he had made a bad decision.

21

It was one of those mean little back streets behind the football ground which the Victorians put up. An endless row of semi-detacheds with outside privies and net curtains in the windows and white washed steps leading up to the front doors. Leafy chestnut trees set in asphalt lined the pavements like well disciplined soldiers on parade, casting their shadows across the road in the hot May sun.

The grocer's shop was on the corner of Paradise Street. Garnett pushed the door open and went inside. He murmured the banal catchphrase to the man behind the counter as he had been instructed to do, and the assistant led him up to the small front room above the shop, and that's all there was to it, except that Vickers was waiting for him. Inevitably he was standing by the window.

He advanced on Garnett with a warm smile on his face and his hand outstretched. "My dear Garnett," he said, wringing his hand, "how good to see you again. I can't begin to tell you how much we all appreciate your magnificent show."

He was like a housemaster talking to the head boy who had just saved the match with an unbeaten century.

"It was a failure," Garnett said, in a voice which was almost inaudible. "I'm told we lost a total of nine men, and what did we achieve? Nothing. We brought out a dead man."

Vickers raised one eyebrow. "Listen to me," he said. "You broke into their maximum security prison and you came out again. You killed one Major General, fifty-four soldiers, a prison governor and six warders. Ten prisoners followed you out through the wall and three of them are still at large. You have rekindled pride in the hearts of many and that by any standard is a victory." An expansive smile flashed across his bloodhound face, "And no hostages were taken, Garnett, because to shoot six thousand people in reprisal would not only have been an admission of defeat, but it would also have driven a great many more people into our camp and that's the last thing they wanted to happen."

"And I made it safe for two hundred and fifty people. Let's not forget that."

"Of course we must not forget that factor in our assessment."

Garnet said, "You're a fucking liar, General, the only people who were in danger were Endicott, Coleman and yourself. And my God what a mess you all made of it. You didn't even know that one of your own subordinates was planning to carry out the job. And then, when Coleman heard there was a possibility that the Stantons had gone across and he didn't know what had happened to Pollard, he was too busy trying to save his own skin to let you know what he was doing. And Endicott? Hell, he was pulling in another direction because, at the time, he didn't know that Pollard was the man whom Special Branch had found in the Swainson's flat. But I'll give you one thing, General, when you took a hand in the business at least you got them all thinking and acting along the same lines. And you were clever. You didn't really hold out much hope that we would be able to bring Pollard out; but you thought that if we came close there was reason to suppose the Russians would give him a whiff of nerve gas, and your little problem would be resolved. And that is where you nearly made a big mistake because they had no such thing in mind, but you were lucky as always, and perhaps that is why you got to be a general."

Vickers said, "I am not going to argue the point with you, Garnett. I weighed the situation up carefully, and in my honest opinion, I came to the conclusion that the Resistance movement could ill afford to lose Coleman, Endicott and myself. However, I did not expect you to agree with my view of things, so it was necessary to convince you that a great many other people were involved. Be honest, if I had told you the truth, would you have done what I asked you to do?"

"I don't know," said Garnett, "it hardly matters now, does it?

190

Nothing matters except Dane. I've tried to get in touch with her, I suppose you know that?"

"As a matter of fact I didn't."

"Where is she?"

"How long have you been in hiding?"

"You know damn well," Garnett said and his voice was tired. "Six weeks and three days."

"I'm afraid she didn't make it."

The colour drained from Garnett's face and he felt as though he had been kicked in the groin. "What do you mean by that?" he said jerkily.

"Someone had to go first and prove the route. You were too valuable so it had to be Dane. We took her to a safe house in Portsmouth where she stayed for about a week, and then, when we were satisfied that the hue and cry had died down, we put her on a train for London. We had her under surveillance the whole time, you understand, and there was nothing, absolutely nothing wrong with her papers, but the night she travelled up to London they made a snap check at the station and she panicked. As a routine precaution we had given her a suicide pill to carry in her mouth. She must have thought they were on to her when they stopped her on the platform and asked to see her papers."

"She killed herself?"

"I'm afraid so."

"Is that all you can say?" Garnett said hoarsely. "I'm afraid she killed herself! God in heaven, you must have had some idea of what that girl had been through. You had no right to let her travel alone, no right at all. Well, you hear this," he said and his voice was shaking, "I'm through. I've had you and Coleman and Endicott right up to my bloody gullet."

He started to move away but Vickers caught hold of his arm. "You can't go like this," he said. "I promised I would get you out of the country and I will. Things are rather difficult at the moment and we have had to close the escape route temporarily but in a month or two we should be able to reopen it. Until it is, I want you to go to this address, 63 Elm Hill, Putney. There is someone there who will

191

look after you until you are your old self again. Have you got that? 63 Elm Hill, Putney."

Garnett shook his arm free. "You can stuff it," he shouted. He turned away, opened the door and ran downstairs.

It was one of those clear, bright, cloudless days which seemed to hold out the promise of a long hot summer. The warm sun was on his back, but he shivered with cold as he limped along the street. He could feel his eyes pricking and there was a lump in his throat and the baying and clapping of the crowd in the football stadium cut across his nerve ends like a band saw. And he could feel the tears welling in the corners of his eyes and he looked up at the sky because he did not want anyone to see him cry.

And there was no escape because he had Vickers' word that the route was closed and there was no Dane to cling on to because he had Vickers' word she was dead. And while Vickers might lie about the impossibility of getting him out of the country because he had other ideas in mind, there was no reason to lie about the girl, was there? And that being so, there was no hope left.

How long, he asked himself, how long must this go on?

And his own words came back to mock him—

"Five, ten, twenty, fifty, or even a hundred years . . . .